The Man Who Would Fly
and other stories

Peter Yorke

The Man Who Would Fly
and other stories

Copyright © 2006 Peter Yorke

The moral right of the author has been asserted.

Apart from any fair dealing for the purposes of research or private study, or criticism or review, as permitted under the Copyright, Designs and Patents Act 1988, this publication may only be reproduced, stored or transmitted, in any form or by any means, with the prior permission in writing of the publishers, or in the case of reprographic reproduction in accordance with the terms of licences issued by the Copyright Licensing Agency. Enquiries concerning reproduction outside those terms should be sent to the publishers.

Matador
9 De Montfort Mews
Leicester LE1 7FW, UK
Tel: (+44) 116 255 9311 / 9312
Email: books@troubador.co.uk
Web: www.troubador.co.uk/matador

ISBN 1 905237 99 5

Typeset in 11pt Stempel Garamond by Troubador Publishing Ltd, Leicester, UK

Matador is an imprint of Troubador Publishing Ltd

For my Father

Thomas S. Yorke
22nd. October 1914 – 31st. December 2005

who would have absolutely understood how and why

Contents

The Man Who Would Fly	1
Supermarket Clash	9
The Big Night	15
Gentleman of the Road	27
No Cornflakes	35
Boys will be Boys	43
Doing the Right Thing	53
The Dogmatic Philosopher	59
The Red Scarf	67
The Final Answer	73
Disappearing Summer	81
In at the Deep End	87
The Sweet Smell of Scorn	95
The Brown Paper Package	97
The Wonders of Education	105

The Man Who Would Fly

Paul Gascoigne sat on the park bench, in the shade of a beech tree. Every day – weather permitting – he ate his lunch here, watching life pass by. Thirty six years old and single, he lived with his parents. He was no trouble and more than paid his way. They just wished that he would find someone and settle down. Every day since leaving school, Paul had travelled on the Underground, from their home in West Harrow into London. He worked at the Ministry of Transport, as a senior clerical officer in the accounts department.

He enjoyed walking, having joined the Ramblers' Association years ago, and was on his local branch committee. A non-driver who had never travelled abroad, he always took his annual holidays with his parents at the same cottage in Bognor Regis. He didn't smoke and drank only a sociable pint of beer or glass of wine. His one vice, a fifty pence permutation on his father's weekly pools coupon. He had won a few thousand pounds a couple of years ago, most of it went on 'doing up' their house.

Six foot tall, medium build, his brown hair and eyes added to his normality. He wore suits with white shirts and plain ties during the week. At the weekend, he preferred roll-necked jumpers and sports jackets. He wore sensible brogues all the time. As tidy in his habits as in his dress, his mother put it down to his profession.

Paul had no experience when it came to women. It wasn't that he didn't like them. The opportunity to get to know any had, over the years, been minimal. Those who knew him, felt he was awkward around women. Only his mother really held out any hope.

The girl who came into his life that day, was stunningly beautiful. Svelte, with a halo of auburn hair, her skin was the colour of peaches. As she came closer, Paul saw that her eyes were silver-grey. Her cream coloured silk dress flowed with her body as she walked. Arriving at his bench, she smiled and sat down. Paul couldn't take his eyes off her. After several minutes, she turned towards him.

'Hello,' she smiled.

'Hello.' Someone had spoken to her. Was it him? He started to apologise. 'I am sorry if I appear t–'

'I'm Helen, isn't it a lovely–'

When two people start speaking at the same time, they usually stop together. Paul felt completely at ease with her. In no time at all, they were chatting like old friends. All too soon it was time to return to his office. For just a moment he considered staying here with this beautiful creature. Then years of discipline took over.

'I must go.'

'Me too,' said Helen.

Without another word, they went their separate ways. Paul was back at his desk, when he realised that she didn't know his name.

By lunch-time the next day, he was a wreck. He'd eaten nothing for dinner the evening before, and barely slept. Only one cup of tea for breakfast. His mother worried that he was sickening for something.

He entered the park, and walked towards his bench. No, now it was their bench. He never doubted that she would return. She wouldn't let him down, and she didn't. She was already there. Today, she had on a blue cotton summer dress, her hair tied with a matching scarf. They talked about everything and nothing. Paul was surprised how interested she was in him, asking questions all the time. He found nothing out about her. The hour flew by. Unable to face another sleepless night he asked if she would be here tomorrow. She said yes. Helen walked away and he waited, his heart on hold. Would she look back? She did, with a smile and an imperceptibly nod of her head.

Paul returned to his office, his thoughts on the next day – Friday. What was he going to do over the weekend? By Friday lunch time he had decided. He had read somewhere, that people should live for the moment. He wasn't completely certain what that meant, but he would give it a try.

'I know you'll think me old fashioned, but I like things well ordered. Everything in its place, do you know what I mean?'

'There is nothing wrong with that,' Helen replied. 'Its just – no, it's not for me to say.'

'What do you mean?' Paul wasn't sure where his words and ideas were coming from. 'Tell me, I value your opinion.'

'You're content with your life, but you can change things if you want to. For example, you could fly if you wish.'

Paul blushed; now he would have to tell her that he had never been in a plane. He really didn't want to.

'Not an aeroplane,' Helen laughed as she spoke. 'I mean fly yourself, free.'

'Of course, I understand.' He felt stupid that he'd misunderstood her. 'You mean metaphorically.'

'No, actually I mean fly. Just flap your wings, you can go anywhere you want to go.'

He spent the weekend thinking about that. As hard as he tried though, he couldn't understand what Helen meant. On the Sunday, he walked with the Ramblers. Over lunch he confided about Helen to a close friend. He told him in no uncertain terms, 'you're in love, Paul'.

By lunch-time on Monday, he'd decided to trust Helen. If at all possible, he would fly with her. He was relieved when she appeared, walking towards the bench. He thought again, how little he knew about her. Where she lived, her job. He would find out today. But first – flying.

'Have you had a good weekend?' Helen asked, as she sat down.

'Yes, thank you. Very nice.' He didn't want small talk. His mind was made up, he wanted to get on with it. 'Can we fly. What do I have to do?'

'Nothing, just take my hand.'

'You don't mean here.' Paul was stunned. 'People will see. Surely we have to go somewhere?'

'Trust me. No-one will see. Just give me your hand.'

Paul did trust her, though it wouldn't have mattered one way or the other. He was completely besotted. He'd walk through fire for her. Taking her hand was easy. Doing it here in public worried him. But what the heck. He reached for her hand.

For the next few moments he floated free of himself. Everything was a haze. He could feel her hand, but nothing else made sense. Then they were back on the bench.

'That was amazing. How did you do that? Where did we go? Did these people see us?'

She laughed at his excitement, 'Do you always ask

so many questions?'

'No, because that sort of thing doesn't happen to me on a regular basis. Just tell me, why didn't anybody see us?'

'It will take me forever to explain. Simply, it's our business not theirs. Therefore, they can't see us.' He was none the wiser. Stunned by what had just happened, he looked into her eyes. 'Can we fly again, soon?'

Helen smiled and got up to leave.

Paul looked at his watch. His lunch hour had gone, he hadn't even eaten his sandwiches. He got up from the bench. ' Well, when can we fly again?"'

'Tomorrow, if you want to.'

Over the next few days, they met and flew every lunch time. Paul thought that his heart would burst, he was so happy. He wanted to tell someone what was actually happening to him. He didn't because Helen asked him not to. Then one day, a couple of weeks after they had first flown, he decided he didn't want to fly today. He wanted some answers instead.

'Of course, if that is what you want,' Helen said, when he told her.

'Do we actually fly, or is it all in my mind?'

'We actually fly.'

'Could I fly on my own?'

'Yes, if you really want to.'

'So when we are up there, if I let your hand go, would I still fly?'

'No. You would be lost in time, dead if you like.' Helen spoke quietly, watching his reaction to her words. 'It's your time; but the flight is mine. It must be your flight, for you to go alone.'

Paul listened to everything Helen said, but was only hearing what he wanted to hear.

'Where do we go when we fly?'

'Nowhere as such. We just move in time.'

'Where in time?'

'To various places in your past.'

'You said it was your flight, so why is it my past? Why not yours?'

'I'm simply acting as your guide to your own past.'

'I don't recognise it."

'That's probably because you were not being sufficiently aware at the time it was happening to you.'

Paul considered that answer very carefully. 'I understand. That part of my past just sort of 'passed me by'. I sort of saw it all, without actually seeing it.'

'Yes, put simply, that is exactly right.' Helen smiled.

He looked at her, and realised that she knew exactly what he was about to ask next. He still asked it. 'Can you control where we go? Could we go forward in time?'

'If that's what you want.'

'Somewhere specific, somewhere I know?'

'Yes, of course.'

'What about going forward twenty four hours. To my home. I could see what's happening, then tomorrow–,' he spoke quickly, almost babbling with excitement. She held up her hands to stop him, and laughed.

'Paul, the only limits on your actions, are all in your mind. If you want to see into the future, then take my hand and you will. Remember though, just as you mustn't change the past, so you can't change the future. It hasn't happened yet, so it isn't susceptible to change. You can only observe what will happen.'

'Will people be able to see us, in the future?'

'You yes; but only if you want them to. It's your

future. They will not see me though.'

'You might be in my future. Surely my future knows that?' Paul spoke hopefully.

'Yes, it does know that of course. If and when I am part of it, we'll travel together, meeting people we both know. Now, at the moment, your future's full of people who don't know me. I have no place there, yet.'

'Then, I don't want them to see me either. Come on; lets do it.' He took her hand.

'Remember, don't let go of me, or you will be lost in time. Unable to return.' Helen smiled at him as she spoke.

'That isn't a problem,' he replied, smiling back. 'I never want to let go of you, anyway.'

Over the last few days, their flights had become more controlled. Paul was better aware, and so more appreciative of what he saw. Now, straight away he recognised the front room of his house. He could hear voices in the kitchen. He was surprised to see the curtains were drawn. The sun was shining through the material. He looked back at Helen and smiled. For some reason, he felt in control. Holding her hand tightly, he led her through to the kitchen.

As they entered the room, Paul saw both his parents sitting opposite one another, at the kitchen table. His mother was crying. Mr. Gascoigne stared blankly at a piece of paper he was holding. It was obviously the cause of their distress. He was speaking quietly to his wife.

'Apparently, he was just sitting there. He used the same bench every day, weather permitting.'

Paul drew Helen around the table, so that he could see over his fathers shoulder. What was Dad looking at? If I could just see what it is, maybe I could do something about it, he thought. He leant down close to his father, and read his own death certificate. The shock of seeing what was written, made him forget everything Helen had said to him. Letting go of her hand, he reached for the paper.

Supermarket Clash

'Hey! Miss. You can't leave your car there.'

Startled by the abrasive tone of the voice, I looked around. Well I mean, you don't expect parking restrictions at 4 am, in a twenty-four hour supermarket car park.

A yellow water-proof clad individual came out of the rain, into the cold white light under the entrance canopy.

'You can't leave your car there,' he repeated, breathless from his excursion through the storm. 'It's handicapped only.'

This could be fun. I'd stopped off to shop, on my way home from a double shift at the local hospital, but there was always time for a laugh.

'I know it's past its best, but my car is not handicapped, I'll have you know.'

He didn't get it; this was not going to be fun. He stared at me for a moment with glazed eyes, then repeated, 'It's handicapped only.'

Of course, I completely understood. However, with wind and rain slanting in from the next parish, the twelve handicapped parking spaces were fairly well protected by the building. My car was the only one here, or for that matter, in the whole car park.

'If anyone more needy comes along, I'm inside. Call me, I'll come straight out and move it.' I didn't anticipate a problem, so leaving him looking aghast, I collected a trolley and went inside.

The evocative smell of fresh baked bread was warm and welcoming, even the musak was okay. As far as I could see, except for a couple of checkout girls the place was all mine. How do they make a profit?

Passing the in-store café, I headed for 'Fruit and Veg'. I harvested potatoes, salad and bananas. Looking back, I noticed that the officious chap from outside had come in from the storm. He was talking to the girls and they were all looking my way.

Oh well, if they have nothing else to do. I moved on, adding some chicken breasts and pork chops to the trolley. Bread and a slab of fruit cake followed.

Well organised people make shopping lists; I'm more your inspirational shopper. Living alone, I don't plan meals, rather I try to surprise myself. So it was, that I was browsing through canned soups, when the lights flickered. Not surprising really with a storm like tonight's, I thought.

I reached for a tin of condensed tomato soup and felt something brush the back of my hand. Snatching it away I looked at the shelf – nothing. Maybe I'd have chicken soup instead. This time as I picked up a tin, something dry and rough grabbed my wrist. Hanging on to the tin I tried to pull free.

What appeared to be a thin plant root was coiling around my wrist. I pulled sharply and broke it. I was free. Holding onto the trolley, I ran out of that aisle and around into 'Desserts'.

A much bigger root was creeping, thickening and spreading out to fill the aisle ahead. 'Back you go, girl.' I speak to myself when I'm alone and scared. Back was blocked off too. I was grabbed around the waist by a more substantial root. I screamed. Other roots caught hold of my legs, then my arms. I screamed again. Don't ask why, I was still hanging onto the trolley, struggling to free it as well as myself.

The roots, whatever they were, pushed me against the shelving. I was in 'Yoghurt and Cream'. Pushing again much harder shattered pots and cartons and covered me with dairy products. I screamed wordlessly.

I was cut and bruised, I watched as more strands started down from the ceiling, It was a struggle to breathe as the roots began wrapping around my chest. I shouted for help again but to no avail. I was going to have to sort this out for myself. Right.

Still I clutched the trolley, my heart beating nineteen to the dozen. I was being slowly pulled into the kitchen section. I looked around and saw cooking utensils. By pulling wildly at the roots, I was able to manoeuvre myself across to a rack, where I grabbed hold of a large chef's knife.

'Now lets see who's boss,' I shouted aloud.

Hacking and stabbing at the roots around me, I gradually managed to cut myself free. Liberating the trolley first, I took a few minutes more to slash a path out of the aisle. Bursting clear, I thought how appropriate the music was – Tom Jones singing 'Please release me'.

Being a nurse, I knew I was needing some first aid. Several large cuts were bleeding profusely, my left wrist felt broken and my ribs hurt. My trolley and I rushed past 'Wines and Spirits' and round towards the checkouts. There I stopped dead, horrified to find the whole area completely filled with the roots.

They were emerging from everywhere and of course, they had followed me. I had absolutely nowhere left to go. I stood still gasping painfully for breath. Stubbornly, I still held on the trolley handle, with the chef's knife in the other hand. Why the trolley? Don't ask, I haven't the foggiest idea.

What little space there was around me, disappeared rapidly. The roots were grabbing at me again. For the first time I noticed a rustling noise that seemed to enhance their threat. Some of them were thorny and when they caught me, the damage inflicted was much more painful. I screamed once more. Surely someone must hear me, I was so near the checkouts.

Now the whole mood of the thing changed, as if it knew I couldn't help myself any more. More roots began to appear, thickening the mass which by now had encircled me completely. Steadily they closed in until finally, I couldn't move at all. I felt as if I was a part of the whole bulk. The pressure increased on my chest and I felt myself beginning to drift into unconsciousness.

Then I saw two glazed eyes peering at me from within the mass and I sensed more than heard a voice say, 'now you'll be eligible to park in the handicapped spaces'.

The in-store café was warm and empty but for me. I looked up and saw a smiling waitress. Behind her was 'Psychotic' from the car park. He was smiling too, if you could call his inane smirk a smile.

'You all right, dear?' she asked. 'you look as if you've seen a ghost.'

Answering with a confidence that I didn't feel, I replied. 'Yes. I'm fine – thanks.' A quick glance at my watch – 4.45 am – how did I get in here? An empty shopping trolley stood beside the table. How did I really feel? Fine.

'Would you like me to get you a fresh coffee?' the

smiling waitress asked. For the first time I noticed a half empty cup, on the table in front of me.

'No, thanks all the same. I'll get on with my shopping.'

I bought some fruit and veg, meat, bread and cake. Then, and it's a strange thing, but I resolutely decided against picking up any tinned soups that night.

The Big Night

The man strode across the beach, the soft sand crunching underfoot. He bent forward into the stiff breeze that blew off the sea. Two fishing rods bounced on his shoulder in time to his stride. His bright yellow, PVC trousers and jacket gave a flash of colour to the otherwise drab foreshore. Black rubber wader boots squeaked and slapped against his thighs. A large knapsack hung on the opposite shoulder from the rods; a paraffin lamp swung in time with his pace from his right hand.

The crescent shaped beach sloped up from the water's edge, to granite cliffs that rose, grey and cold towards an overcast sky. He walked to the end of the beach where, at the bottom of the tide, he'd be able to wade round into an adjacent cove. Because this was the only access, the cove was rarely visited except by an occasional fisherman. A small flock of oyster catchers screeched as they flew along the water's edge.

He looked at his watch and smiled. An hour to dusk, two to low tide; four hours fishing ahead. Reaching the end of the beach he watched the breakers, then judging the moment, he waded round into the cove.

Leaving the water he walked up the beach. A large rock stood in the middle of the cove. High above, seagulls rose from the cliff top, screaming in protest at his intrusion. Carefully he stood the two rods against the wet, grey rock. The bag and lamp went on a ledge, five feet up on the rock. Looking back at the receding tide, he took a hand rolled cigarette from a tin and lit it. He drew the acrid smoke into his lungs, watching the waves breaking thirty yards away.

The water was cold, grey and foreboding. White topped breakers showed dark green bases momentarily, before they crashed onto the beach. The wind carried spray from each wave into the cove. The man wasn't concerned, he was dressed for it. He turned to look up at the cliffs. A flash of pink from a clump of thrift caught his eye. He marvelled at the plant's ability to grow in such a hostile environment.

The cigarette finished, he walked up the beach towards the base of the cliff, and entered a small cave, it's entrance almost invisible behind rocks. From a high shelf ten yards in, he took some bamboo poles left from previous visits. Lashed together in threes, they provided tripod supports for his rods.

He first came to this cove as a small boy with his father. He'd watched in wonder as silver fish twisted and strained in the surf, fighting to be free of hook and line. Over the years, with others and alone, he had returned many times to catch sea bass.

He had many memories: of the night he'd caught eight fish all over six pounds, or the fifteen pound giant, that he'd waded into the surf to grab. This was the magnet that drew him to this place, the magic that spread through his soul. He was certain, one day he would hook the one fish in a million, so quenching his greatest need.

He prepared both rods; one with a shock leader and six ounce weight that he would cast as far as possible, out over the breakers. The other he rigged with a break away weight, to catch in the sand like an anchor. This he'd cast into the surf. Both hooks were baited with green peeler crabs, soft smelly morsels that tempted bass round here like no other bait.

He'd gathered them that morning, from beneath pieces of old carpet, laid on the mud in the estuary near to his home. The crabs needed shelter when shedding their shells made them vulnerable to predators.

The man whistled tunelessly as he fastened a crab to each hook with some elastic cotton. Then, picking up one rod and a tripod, he walked down the beach. Wading into the surf up to his thighs, he cast long and flat to the back of the breakers. Backing out from the water, more line running from the reel, he reached the beach where he rested the rod against the bamboo tripod and took in slack line.

After casting the second rod he glanced at his watch. He'd been here for half an hour; coffee time. The hot, sweet liquid scorched and roughened his tongue. He wrapped his hands round the plastic flask cup for warmth and watched his rods. Years of fishing from here had taught him the best time. Across the bay, high water brought the fish in under the harbour wall. Here, low tide was best as it retreated across the shallow hollows and ridges on the sand. All his significant catches had been around dusk, at low tide and from this beach.

Taking a small jar of methylated spirit from his bag, he primed then lit the lamp. The warm, sweet smell of the meths enveloped him, followed by the more pungent odour of burning paraffin as the mantle came alight. Instantly, dusk turned black outside the ring of light. He pressurised the lamp, finished his drink and went to check the rods.

The one fishing the breakers was tight, and moving rhythmically with the surf. The other had gone slack, the wind tugging the line in a huge arc. He tightened up until he could feel the weight again and reset the rod on its stand. A picture of the bait rolling invitingly on the sea bed, formed in his minds eye. He imagined a huge fish moving slowly towards it. Back at his bag, he selected and lit another cigarette, then checked his watch. The tide would turn soon.

He was by the rock when the rod fishing behind the breakers started to quiver. He saw the luminous tip waggle and reached it in seconds. Winding in slack line, he eased the rod back. A steady jerking told him he had a fish on. He struck slowly and smoothly. Then, reeling in line all the time, he walked into the surf. He raised the twelve foot rod high above his head, trying to pull the fish's head up. Then, winding the tip back down, he retrieved more line. Not big he thought, seeing the first flash of silver in the surf. A few moments passed and a three pound bass lay in the pool of lamp light.

The man removed the hook gently. He carefully weighed the fish on a portable scale, measured it's length and girth with a flexible ruler, then took it back to the sea. After holding it in the water for a moment to revive it, he released it into the creamy surf. Hands rinsed off, he went back to the rod, baited up again and recast. Returning to the rock, he removed a slim book and pencil from the bag. Details of the fish joined the already long list.

They always went back, it had been a long time since he'd eaten one. It didn't seem right to treat the monarch of the surf that way. Friends said he was crazy, with restaurants paying really good prices for sea bass. He saw it as his contribution towards helping guarantee the fish stock and his sport for a little longer. He often wondered if he'd caught any fish more than once; whether they had lain on the sand looking up, recognising him as a past victor.

Smiling at the thought, he looked at his watch and was surprised to see he'd been there for ninety minutes, thirty to low tide. He retrieved the second rod, changed the bait, and recast out into the surf table behind the fourth breaker. Then, he poured some more coffee.

It was now quite dark. He stood by the two rods, looking along the curve of the bay. The harbour was bright with necklaces of orange and white lights, which flickered and winked in the mist of the spray blown off the surf. He shivered slightly, though he wasn't cold. That didn't stop him from stamping his feet on the sand. For the next hour he fished, smoked and drank coffee.

A three-quarter moon rose, adding its cold, white light to the black-grey background. Rock corners became stark, sharp shapes, for the mind to conjure into images. He re-baited three times in the hour. Now the tide had turned, he moved the rods and stands back each time. Looking at the headland – his exit route – he judged he could stay another hour and a half.

At the precise moment he reached for the second rod to change the bait, it pulled towards the sea with tremendous force. He grabbed hold of the rod with both hands. He'd never felt such a pull in all his life. Releasing the bail arm on the reel to let out line, he raised the quivering tip above the skyline, to see when the fish stopped its dash. It had gone off parallel to the beach for some thirty yards, before turning out towards the open sea. The resulting curve in the line gave him a chance. Rushing into the water he started winding in line.

When he next 'felt' the fish he struck hard and firm, at the same time walking backwards, keeping the line taut. He felt the heavy, thudding jerks of a big fish as the hook lodged. Got you. It was off again, back across the beach. By moving along with it and keeping the line tight, he kept it moving parallel to the beach, even gathered more line.

He started to think about what it might be; how best to land it. Tope ran hard, but he'd never heard of one caught from here. He retrieved more line, then the rod tip powered round in a curve. He moved towards the sea, taking some of the pressure off the fish. Conger eels came onto these beaches. No, this fish was too quick; the same for ray and the water was too warm for cod.

He began to consider the possibility that this just might be the night and the place. He'd finally hooked his big bass. He gathered himself both mentally and physically, then started to wind in line. The fish exerted pressure on the line but the hook felt set. Then the rod eased back, the line slackened, the rod tip flicked upright. He froze in disbelief. He'd lost it. The line must have broken, or maybe the shock leader parted.

He visualised the end tackle, considered every swivel and knot. That took just five seconds, then he galvanised into action. Quickly retrieving line, he started to walk backwards up the beach. He was so engrossed, that he tripped over the lamp before realising he'd reached it. The glass and mantle broke, paraffin spread over a small area of beach. He fell into the fire, but rolled away, suffering only singed hair. He kept hold of the rod and now a tugging pull told him he still had the fish.

He laughed aloud. Swim straight in, eh! Thought you'd catch me that easily? He walked down towards the sea still retrieving line. He tried to sense if the fish was tired, but it didn't seem to be. He felt the reel, judging that he had about a hundred feet of line out.

Come on you devil, show yourself. It was just in the breakers, he could feel the swell moving the fish through the rod. Then it broke water in a series of foaming leaps, clearly visible in the moonlight. It was in the creamy water between the second and third breaker. The sight of it stilled him. For several seconds he watched, hardly daring to believing his eyes.

It was a bass. Better, it was the bass that he had hunted all these years. He judged it to be over twenty pounds, and thirty inches long. Its power had astounded him. He just had to land it. It strained at the rod tip again. He gave it line. It went straight out for nearly two hundred feet. To keep in touch, he went back up the beach keeping the line tight, letting it know he was still here.

Then all was still. He returned to the water winding line in all the time, then out up to his thighs. Keeping the rod tip high to hold the fish's head up, he began slowly reeling it in.

His arms were aching with the strain of the struggle. He tried to look at his watch, but the glass had been blackened in the accident with the stove, he couldn't see the time. He looked across at the headland judging there was time to get this fish out. He continued to wind it in. The fish twisted and pulled, it was not quite tired enough just yet. The fire around the paraffin stove was still alight. He hoped that his bag was all right.

Then, as the fish turned to the beach again, the line slackened and a wave knocked him off balance. Water closed over him, he was kneeling on the bottom. Scrambling upright, blinded by the water in his eyes, he realised that he hadn't got the rod. Looking down at the water, he tried to see into it's inky blackness but it was no good. Shivering with a cold that was both physical and mental, it slowly dawned on him, he'd lost the fight.

He thought about the fish still attached to the rod. Would it dislodge the hook, now that the pressure was off the line? He stumbled out of the water, his waders full, his clothes wet and cold. He looked seawards and silently vowed to the fish that there would be another day.

He turned his attention to the present. Removing his waders, emptying them as he did, he then took off his socks, rung them out and then put them back on. Wiping the glass of his watch, he was surprised to see that over an hour and a half had passed since the tide turned. He must get off the beach, quickly.

He packed his tackle bag, cooled the hot lamp in a rock pool, and was pleased to see that it had mostly survived the fire. A new glass, a mantle and a coat of paint and it would be as good as new.

He was pulling the first boot back on, when he was amazed to see the other one start to slide, back down towards the sea. He watched it for several seconds, before realising what was happening. As he had walked out of the sea, the boot must have got caught up in the line. Now, all he had to do, was follow it back to find his rod, and maybe, even the fish.

He untangled the wader, and put it back on. He started back towards the sea, feeling his way along the line with both hands. He walked into the water and straight away, felt the fish tugging on his left hand. Feeling down the line he found the rod in a couple of feet of water. He rinsed the sand from the reel, pleased to feel it was working quite well. A minute later he was back in contact with the fish.

His heart leapt with pure joy. He didn't notice his wet clothes, or feel the cold any more. Again, he tried to judge how much line was out and exactly where the fish was. He raised the tip high and straight away felt the now familiar, steady pull.

'You're tiring aren't you?' The first words that he had spoken aloud all evening, echoed around the cove. He backed up the beach, rod held high, until he had almost reached the cliffs.

Looking at his other rod, he saw the handle was already under water. Backing towards the sea retrieving line, he drew level with it. Cutting its line with a knife from a belt sheath, he collected the rod and tripod.

Then, back up the beach again, pulling the fish in further, putting them by the rock. Back down to the water, splashing close by told him that victory was his. He went into the surf and in a foot of water he found it, lying on its side.

He recovered the rest of the line, until the rod tip was just a few feet, from the huge head. Moving back a few paces, the fish slid in on the small wavelets. When they returned to the ocean, the bass was finally stranded. It flipped several times, as if to show him that it still had some fight left. Cutting it free of the line, he reached down and hooked the first two fingers of his left hand into the red gill slits. Then, he lifted the fish from the wet sand and carried it and the rod back to the rock.

He realised that the incoming tide was just a few yards away. Looking at the headland, he knew he'd stayed here too long. A glance at his watch confirmed it; he should have left the beach twenty minutes ago. He was cut off. Lighting a cigarette, he drank the last of his coffee, and considered his position.

High tide was in about an hour, it would rise to seven foot deep. No-one had ever climbed right up the cliff, but he could easily get high enough to stay dry. Then it was just a matter of waiting for the tide to go down. Calmly, he set about his preparations.

First, he weighed the fish. He took the scales from his bag, but was reluctant to put the hook in the gills, fearful of damaging such a heavy fish. He took a towel from his bag and placed the fish on it, then wrapped it up and hooked the scales through the material. The needle quivered for a moment, then steadied. In the moonlight he could just make it out. Twenty two pounds fourteen ounces. Gently he lowered it down, standing still for a moment, as if in shock. Then he took the tape; thirty four inches nose to tail. He wrote it up in his book at twenty two pounds, allowing for the towel.

He finished the cigarette, watching the gills pump. No-one will believe me unless they see you. Having made up his mind, he took a priest from the bag, and quickly struck it hard – twice – on its head. The fish was dead. Feeling elated in spite of having killed such a fish, he let out a yell of victory and punched the air.

He began to pack up his tackle. The rods and poles went into the cave, secured to the shelf where he normally left the poles. They would be safe up there, he could collect them tomorrow. He checked the cave, but judged that the water would be three or four feet high right to the back. He wrapped the bass in the towel and then secured it under the top flap of the knapsack.

Studying a part of the cliff that was visible in the moonlight, he located a way up to a ledge well above high water. Gathering his bag and the remains of the lamp, he crossed over to the cliff. The tide had already reached the bottom of his climb.

The first ten feet were wet and slippery and covered with seaweed, but he easily reached the ledge. Now that he was safe, he settled himself down, lit a cigarette and thought over the events of the evening.

He considered the effect that this fish – his fish – would have on the small sea-side village. It could bring plenty of anglers, maybe do us all a bit of good. Wondering if anyone was worrying about him. He thought not. Never having married and with his parents dead, there was just his brother. Neighbours would think he was spending the night away, he often did. Good, no-one to worry.

Trying to make himself a bit more comfortable, he stood up to move along the ledge. Whether he slipped, stumbled over the bag, or missed the edge of the ledge in the darkness, he fell. His right arm caught in the strap of the bag, which went with him. His head struck the front edge of the ledge that he'd chosen for his sanctuary. It was a sickening blow that crushed in the side of his skull. He was dead when he fell into the shallow water that had already covered the beach, so recently the scene of his greatest triumph.

His blood turned the water around him dark in the moonlight. The rising tide lapped around his body and the dead fish strapped in his bag. The victor and the vanquished, now neither of them better off.

Gentleman of the Road

The scorching heat of a July day forced the tramp to walk slowly up through the village. He planned to collect a meal by knocking at some of the cottage doors. Then he would continue, past a small green and up a low hill. There, he could rest in the shade of the trees at the top.

He was certain of someone showing him sympathy. There was a familiarity about the place. He felt sure he had been here before – maybe a long time ago. He approached one cottage, set back within a tidy garden and spotted a woman weeding a flower bed. She heard his boots crunch on the gravel path. Rising up she watched him approach.

She smiled at him, speaking with that same smile in her voice. 'Hello, would you like a drink? You look hot.'

He nodded his thanks, agreeing on a cup of tea. While she was inside the cottage, he gathered up the weeds that lay around and swept the path. When she returned with a tray, he felt that he had earned the drink.

She handed him a mug of tea. 'I knew it was you, I recognised you straight away. Help yourself to sugar, if you take it.' She pointed to the tray carrying a plate of custard creams and a sugar bowl, that she had ballanced on the wall by the gate.

'Recognised me?' He gazed at her intently, looking

for a clue to help his memory. 'I'm sorry, I must seem very rude, but–.' His voice faded rather than ending abruptly.

'You came here picking fruit, most summers back in the early seventies. You did odd jobs for us around the farm as well.'

'I don't remember, sorry.' So, I have been here before he thought. Details were returning slowly, but twenty five years on the road had taught him things. He'd continue playing ignorant. He gazed past the woman out beyond the cottage, but could see only trees.

'Where's the farm?'

'That went many years ago. If you walk up the hill, you'll find a derelict cottage near the top. There's a factory away down on the left. That's built on our old farm land.'

Feeling that she wanted to speak, he decided to open up a little. Thinking intently he said, 'I'm beginning to remember, you were married, where's your husband? Why did you let the land go?'

The woman smiled, 'I knew you would remember. You came here for so many years. My husband disappeared twenty years ago. He went out to put the chickens away in their huts, then to have a 'scout around' as he would put it. We had been having some trouble with a fox that year. He never returned.'

'Where did he go?' he lifted his gaze to watch her as she answered.

'I have no idea. I really wish I did.'

Quietly, she told him the whole story. It appeared that her husband really had disappeared. The police searched every inch of the farm to no avail. They widened the search area, until finally they had checked the whole village, but they found nothing. He had vanished without trace.

'He liked to walk up to the top of the hill, said you could see everything we owned from up there. We don't know if he went that evening, the police searched the old cottage and its garden particularly but there was no sign of him.' A faraway look crossed her eyes as she spoke.

In the beginning there had been sightings all over the country. The police checked them all without success. They told her it was perfectly normal for well meaning people, as well as cranks and attention seekers to claim to have seen him.

Then slowly the sightings became less frequent until finally, they stopped. For the next few years she struggled, trying to keep their farm going. It was a continuous battle against not just the weather, but also the bank and their refusal to understand when times got hard.

'So, after seven years, I had him declared legally dead.' She was speaking calmly now, without passion. 'Then I sold the farm to cover the debts that had built up over those difficult times. I've lived here these past eighteen years, hoping that one day he would...' At last her voice faltered and she looked away to hide her tears.

The old man stood deep in thought. Now he remembered the ginger haired farmer, together with his smiling wife. They worked hard to develop their fruit farm, always showing him kindness.

Finally he trusted himself to speak without emotion; she didn't need that from him, not after all this time. 'I'm sorry. I'm beginning to remember you now. It's with all the changes round here, I barely recognise the place.'

The woman stood still, looking at him intently. Suddenly, she made up her mind. 'You look as if you could do with a proper meal. Maybe a bath, too?'

Both were too old to be embarrassed by her reference to hygiene.

'That would be very nice, thank you.' He couldn't remember the last time that he'd had a hot bath. Usually it was in a stream, were he sometimes emerged smelling worse than when he had gone in.

'Look, why don't you stroll up to the old cottage at the top of the hill. You can see the farm site and the factory. See what they have done over there. I'll get the water hot for your bath, and then we can have dinner.'

'You're very kind, are you sure about this? Suppose your neighbours see.'

'They can just mind their own business,' she snapped. 'I'm sorry, I shouldn't take it out on you. Some of them said hateful things when my husband first disappeared. I really don't give a fig for what any of them say or think.'

He took a small rucksack from his shoulder and then removed an old raincoat. Folding the coat, he placed it carefully on the ground, and put the bag on top. 'Can I leave these here?'

She nodded.

'I'll see you soon.' He turned out through the gate, picking up the few biscuits that remained on the plate. He knew that he'd eat well tonight, but old habits die hard. Seeing his action she smiled slightly to herself, then watched him walk off slowly up the slope. It will be pleasant to have company for a change she thought, turning towards the house.

As he walked, the tramp looked around trying to recall more of his last time here. It was difficult. That's the price of a life on the road. There's little permanency for a travelling man. Nothing on which to hook memories. He could barely picture the farmer – or for that matter his wife – clearly.

It took him just a few minutes to reach the derelict cottage, hidden amongst trees at the top of the hill. The woman was right. The factory site lay like a scar on the rural scene around it. He turned away and opened a gate that hung on a single hinge. He pushed through a jungle of weeds and garden plants that had overgrown with neglect.

Moving round to the rear of the cottage, he came upon a small area surprisingly clear of undergrowth. There was a well in remarkably good condition considering it's obvious age. Looking down into its dark interior, there was no sign of the bottom. Sitting on the wall of the well, he leant back against one of the posts that still held an axle and handle. He took off his dirty, sweat stained trilby, putting it on the wall beside him, then settled back to enjoy the custard creams and the sunshine. Sugary things were not a regular in his diet. These were a real treat indeed. Thinking about the story he'd just heard, he felt sorry for the woman.

He'd met plenty of men, who said they'd walked away from families with insatiable appetites, mortgages, their work. Taking account of his own life back along, when he and others like him were seen as 'Gentlemen of the Road', there where plenty of folk who would find something for him to do around their garden, in return for a few pence, or a bite to eat.

In his time, he'd sharpened knives, mown lawns and cut hedges. He had been a night watchman at road works, laboured on building sites, picked all sorts of fruit and vegetables. In those days, just after the Second World War, tramps weren't viewed in the same way as they are now fifty years on.

'Called up' in 1947, he'd done his stint as an Army cook. 'Lots of luverly grub, that's why', he would always say. Discharged when his two years were up, he went home to find his mother, widowed in the last months of the war, had met someone else and was planning to remarry. His home, that had sheltered him for almost all his life, was no longer welcoming. He was happy for his mother, but he didn't like the man now sleeping in his father's bed. His welcome home had been, 'Call me Phil, yeh. You're a bit too old for Dad'.

No way. Packing his demob suit and a few bits and bobs into a cardboard suitcase, he'd left the only place that – to this day – he'd ever called home. Still under twenty one, he set out along the route of seasonal casual work.

Over the next forty years, he'd never had much. Mind, he hadn't starved – well not for long, anyway. Sure there were hard times, particularly during severe winters. He'd wonder if he was getting wet and cold for too long. He moved into cities in the winter, trying to get warmth from the buildings.

Eating the biscuits while he'd thought of the past, the occasional crumb even a small piece fell into the well. There in the gloom, thirty feet or so below ground level, they attracted a tiny mouse. Out of a crack in the wall, then down onto the flat, empty well floor, it scampered across towards its feast. The floor seemed to give a little shudder and rose imperceptibly. The mouse had gone, absorbed by the floor.

The old man started to nod off in the quiet warmth of this place. Standing up, he stretched for a moment or two. Turning to pick up his hat, he accidentally brushed it down into the well. It dropped onto a ledge some ten feet below the wall. As he looked down he was sure he could reach it. He'd worn it for several years, it was a good servant to him. He wouldn't easily find another as good.

He tried to reach it by just leaning over, but without luck. He would need a stick or something. Looking around, he found an old bamboo cane he thought would do the job, but it wasn't quite long enough. Leaning further over with the bamboo, was his last mistake. He simply over-stretched and quick as a flash he fell without a sound, past his hat and down onto the floor of the well.

The floor engulfed him without knowing what it was devouring. It shuddered for several minutes, then moved up the wall by a couple of feet or more. Settling down to its new level, it waited for more sustenance. That was the most it had grown since long before, when another had come down to it. Without understanding, it had robbed a woman of a man for the second time in her life.

Some day the world would know and suffer. Until that time it would spread upwards, slowly climbing meal by meal, towards the ledge and the hat that lay in the sunshine.

No Cornflakes

It's essential to have bad days, then you can appreciate good days more. For me, last Thursday was a bad day, starting at breakfast. There were no Cornflakes.

'There are no Cornflakes,' I said, shaking the empty box over my empty bowl.

'I've put them on the shopping list,' my wife said from the kitchen.

'What about breakfast today?' I asked, innocently.

'Have something else,' she said.

'What is there?' still innocently, but that was about to stop – quickly.

'Nothing, until I go shopping.' As soon as she'd said it, I'm sure she felt silly.

'I'll just have some coffee.' I went through to help myself.

'We're out of coffee, it's on the list too. Sorry darling.' She stopped loading the washing machine, and looked up. 'Anyway, the kids finished the milk; you couldn't have drunk it black.'

That amounts to some sort of justification? As this household's sole provider, I suppose I shouldn't expect to eat and drink by right.

Leaving the house, I carried a hold-all full of badminton kit. I play after work most Thursday's. Throwing the bag into the boot, I got into the car. It wouldn't start. I looked at my watch – 7.45 am, I was going to be late. Another try, still nothing. Getting out and slamming the door, I started walking to the bus stop.

Money – or rather the lack of it – was the cause of my premature return home. For reasons I won't try to explain, I'd left my wallet on my bedside table.

I finally arrived at the office an hour late. Probably a tad more annoying than being late, was that I hadn't been missed. My secretary was having a day off, as distinct from my off day. My terminal had just stored emails, pending anyone arriving. A quick look at the overnight input, then I went in search of coffee.

A cracked plastic coffee cup is diabolical, not only because you lose the drink, but because the leakage is on your trousers, before you feel it. I went to the men's cloakroom, to try and mop up the worst of the stain. The water from the tap splashed wildly, soaking me even more – and there were no paper towels.

I raced for the privacy of my office, to find the Accounts Director waiting. We had no sartorial common ground, at the best of times. His grey and lilac Austin Reed had nothing in common with my Charity shop look. It's to his everlasting credit that we talked business, without him once commenting upon my appearance. Some might say his phraseology was full of innuendos; leakage, flow, trickle and seepage, are not words that he normally used when discussing departmental financial performance, whether good or bad. His backward glance from the doorway as he left was minimalist.

I locked the door and draped my trousers, jacket and shirt over the hot radiator. I anticipated they would need about half an hour to dry. I sat down to work. Ten minutes later the window cleaner's platform rose into view. Of course, Thursday, window cleaning day. I wondered how many office blocks in London, had female window cleaners.

I normally lunch in the park, weather permitting. A sandwich, or a burger with a drink, usually hits the spot. Today, for obvious reasons, I didn't risk another plastic cup. That's why my friend Danny, found me with a drink can in one hand, the ring minus the pull bit, in the other. The drink was still firmly locked in.

Danny reached across. 'Give it to me, you lummox.' I had been telling him about my day. 'I think I had better open it.' He had a Swiss army knife – honestly. He located a suitable implement, and set about my can. It's beyond me, quite how I was the one that got soaked in the foaming liquid that spurted forth, when Danny broke into the can.

Funny how events can affect our thinking. Synonymous with the arrival of the latest fluid assault upon me, I remembered I'd left my badminton kit in the car boot. Having said a fond farewell to Danny, I went to ring my wife, from a public call box.

I didn't spot the brown paper bag at first. After all, it was right there on the shelf beside the 'phone. I made my call, arranging for my kit to be dropped at reception, when she came shopping. Then, I noticed the bag.

The paper bag held a plastic bag, full of plaster of Paris. Looking around, no-one seemed interested. I threw it away in a adjacent waste bin. Heading back to my office, I didn't see a young lad, retrieve the bag and start after me. I did hear a squeal of tyres, that heralded the arrival of a car at the call box. Looking back, I saw two large men get out. They seemed angry. I made a point of telling the reception desk that my wife would leave a hold-all.

Compared to the morning, my afternoon was uneventful. Of course, I had to spend fifteen minutes, drying the cola soaked shirt. The photo copier did run out of paper; and sometime, I really must pull the filing cabinet off the wall. Then I could gather the couple of hundred paper clips, that fell down the back of it, around 3.30.

By 5.00 I was ready for off. They had my hold-all at reception. As he handed it over, the duty security man, mumbled something about a lad's parcel. I thanked him, ignored what he said, and headed out into the rush hour. The sports hall's about a mile from my office. I usually drive, when I've a performing car.

Today, I walked. I hadn't seen the lad following me at lunch time. Now I didn't see the two men trailing me. Actually, four people were following me, though the second pair were tailing the first pair, not me.

Arriving at the sports hall, I booked in. We are a casual group on Thursday evenings, playing whoever turns up. I went to change, having seen several people down by the courts. When I opened the hold-all, I saw the paper bag.

At first I thought, that my wife's conscience had been pricked, and had made me a sandwich. When I opened it, I recognised the bag of plaster again. That was when I became aware that someone was following me.

'We'll 'ave that, guv,' a voice spoke from behind me. I turned, to find the two men I'd seen at lunchtime. They had looked big then – close up they were enormous.

'You've followed me here, for some bag of plaster. I'm amazed.' I carried on changing.

One of them pulled me upright, by my hair. It was

about to get even nastier, when a voice spoke from behind them.

'That's quite enough of that. All of you, stand against the wall.'

The voice turned out to be the police. They took all of us to the local station, and put us in three cells. After a couple of hours, I was taken to an office to meet two officers, who said their names were D S Harris, and D C Stanley.

They asked me how I knew the twin rocks, and where I got the paper bag. I told them about the events of midday. They didn't understand why I was in such a dishevelled state, and asked if I was sleeping rough. My real problem though, was not having an answer, for how the paper bag was in my hold-all.

'If you ring my wife, she will tell you that she brought my hold-all to work for me. And I'm sure my company's security, will tell you when I picked it up.'

Harris replied, 'we've tried to talk to your wife sir, but there's no reply at your home.'

'Of course not, she's probably still shopping.' I thought about how long she might be. 'You've got my watch, what's the time?'

'8.40,' Harris said. That floored me, I'd lost all sense of time. She should have been home hours ago.

'Could you try her again?' I asked quietly.

'We have someone waiting outside your house, sir.' Harris looked at a file he'd brought in with him. 'They will let us know, the instant she gets home.'

Something struck me as odd. 'What's so important about a bag of plaster? What is it, Elgin Marble dust?'

The two detectives looked at each other. 'You really don't know do you?' Stanley spoke for the first time.

I looked at him for a moment, 'Officers. I don't know

anything; I've been trying to explain that for the last twenty minutes.'

Harris looked at me for a moment. 'The bag doesn't contain plaster, sir. It's a kilo of uncut heroin.'

That was when I asked for my solicitor to be called. They put me back in the cell. Gordon Blake, who up until today had conveyed a couple of houses for us, and organised my will, arrived in no time. We talked, and forty minutes later he had me bailed, to appear back here in three weeks time.

'My car doesn't start, and I end up a drug dealer,' I said to him as he drove me home. I looked at my recovered watch, 10.30 pm. The house was in darkness; where was everyone? Then I went cold, she's left me, and taken the kids I thought. She thinks that I'm a criminal. I let myself in, and went through to the kitchen.

The note was in the middle of the kitchen table. I really didn't want to read it, but what the heck. It would finish this horrendous day off perfectly. I read;

Hi. Hope you got your bag. I've had your car fixed, the cam belt or something, the chap from the garage said. The kids fancied a film, so we've gone into town. There's a shepherds pie in the 'fridge, microwave it for five minutes on high.
Luv u. xxx

I sat down at the kitchen table thinking about the last fifteen hours. I would laugh I thought, if it wasn't all so sad. I put on a pot of coffee, set the microwave for the pie, then went upstairs for a quick shower.

At work the following day, I was a celebrity. Comments ranged from, 'can you fix me up for the weekend?' to 'I'll visit you if you go down.' Mid morning and the security man who'd been on the front desk yesterday afternoon, came up to tell me what had happened.

'This youngster followed you in, but you were already in the lift. He said you'd dropped the package. I stuck it under the desk as we were busy. When your wife brought the hold-all in, I thought I'd do you a favour. So I put the bag in.'

'Did you get a name for this kid?' I asked.

He shrugged and shook his head. 'Sorry.'

My secretary vowed that she would never take another day off, unless I did too. 'You can't be left alone can you?' she said. 'Do you want a coffee?'

Today turned out fine – good even. Tame drinks, tantrum free taps, and a car that worked. Plus, most importantly, Cornflakes for breakfast. Maybe that's what is really needed, Cornflakes for breakfast.

I walked down into the foyer at five o'clock heading for home, and the weekend. The security man who had spoken to me earlier was at the desk. He beckoned me over.

'I think your off the hook, sir,' he said. 'I made a statement to the police this afternoon. They sort of hinted, it would see you all right. Is there anything else I can do for you?'

'No thank you,' I said. 'You've done quite enough already.' Halfway to the door I stopped. 'On second thoughts, there is something. Have you got a phone number for the window cleaners?'

Boys will be Boys

Despite being brothers, Peter and Paul Wilson might as well have been born to different families. They bore no resemblance to one another in word or deed.

Peter, the older by fifty one weeks, never missed an opportunity to point it out. Tall for his age with dark hair and complexion, he took after his matriarchal Grandma, who forever sang or read to them.

Two little sparrows sitting on a wall,
One named Peter the other named Paul.
Fly away Peter; fly away Paul.
Come back Peter, come back Paul.

Peter was athletic, a doer and the leader. Paul, fair and slight like his Dad, wasn't exactly bright, but enjoyed school. He worked hard at his lessons and was rewarded for his efforts with good average marks. Peter roughed him up when they played together; too often for the younger boy to like his older brother. He kept quiet because he feared worse if he spoke out. They had little to do with each other, until they were eleven, when their Dad's new job moved them into the country.

The new house was on the edge of a small market town, at the end of a lane. 'If anyone comes this far, they're looking for us,' Mum said, on moving day. The boy's were happy with separate bedrooms, chickens in the garden and an orchard with several different fruit's.

'This could be okay,' Peter said to Paul, as they, kept out of the way of the removal men. They hadn't wanted to leave the old house and their friends. 'It's not bad, I suppose,' replied Paul. They discovered the enormous garden, that was surrounded on all sides by huge fields, some grass, others with crops. Later that evening, as they all explored, Dad said they were peas, and barley.

'What's barley for, Dad?' asked Paul.

'You make beer with it and all sorts,' Dad replied. 'Look here you two,' he went on, 'you're to keep out of the fields, damaging crops. Stay in the garden, there's plenty enough room for you to play.'

Their new school proved better than they had anticipation. Paul quickly settled in, having found himself 'well up' academically. Peter scored three goals in his first break-time football game. Third 'pick' for a team that afternoon, he was in heaven. The school bus had barely reversed away, having dropped them at the top of the lane, before they had raced into the kitchen, both talking 'nineteen to the dozen', telling their smiling mother the details of their first day.

She hugged them both, laughing out loud. 'Calm down both of you. Are you the Peter and Paul that didn't want to go this morning? Come on both of you, upstairs and change. Yes, you can play out until tea time. Dad will be home soon, we'll have tea together. Slow down, walk up stairs quietly, and fold your school clothes, please.' She smiled as they went upstairs. 'Thank goodness,' she thought, 'the biggest problem with this move looks to have been sorted out.'

Tea had been a happy meal. Sausage, eggs and chips with bread and butter, then tinned peaches and evaporated milk for pudding. Everyone had a story to tell, and laughter rang out. Later they went with their Dad, to 'sort out the chickens'.

Mum had boiled up potato peelings, mixed it with bran and eggshells. She brought it out in a white enamel bucket.

'Why do you put shells in their food, Mum?' said Paul, as he filled a trough with the sweet smelling mash.

'To help them make shells for the eggs that they lay,' she replied. Looking at him, she was surprised he was satisfied with that answer.

Peter helped his Dad fix a piece of hose from a tap by the old tool shed at the bottom of the garden. They tucked the other end into another trough and turned the tap on. 'Good, Peter my boy. Now if we turn the tap on for a couple of minutes each day, the chickens will have water.'

'Can I do that Dad? Please say that I can, I'll never forget, I promise.'

His father agreed ruffling Peter's hair. 'I suppose you can, if you want to.'

He smiled across at his wife, who nodded slightly. Later, with the two boys sound asleep, they talked about their day, pleased that everything had settled down so quickly.

Over the following weeks, Peter and Paul stopped being 'new boy's' at school. When the summer holiday's came round, they'd forgotten their past life. Most evenings and weekends, they played out. With their father's help, they turned the garden shed into a den. Occasionally, their mother packed them a picnic, then they'd stay out there all day. She didn't mind. From the back door she could hear the hum of their voices; she always knew where they were.

Things weren't all that they seemed. They were

getting on a bit better, but Paul still got the thin end of everything. Peter was ever the leader no matter what they were playing. Peter didn't punch quite as much, but Paul remembered.

On the last day of school, the bus dropped them as usual and they stood by the road, watching it disappear back down the lane. 'Eight weeks,' said Peter smiling broadly. 'Eight whole weeks without rotten old school.' They turned to walk down the path to their house.

'I think I'll get bored,' Paul said, pulling a stem of grass, and chewing the soft pulpy end.

'I won't,' replied Peter, 'there's loads to do. Lets play explorers tomorrow, I'll be Captain Cook.' Paul asked what he would be. 'You can be first mate, like that story we're reading at school.'

'What, Mr. Christian, is that the one?' Peter nodded, Paul smiled to himself at Peter's ignorance.

The following day they set out, with sandwiches, biscuits and a bottle of lemonade, to find what was to be found. 'Back for tea,' Mum said, checking Paul had his watch. At breakfast Dad laid down some rules for the holidays, particularly after he had heard their plans for that day. 'I've told you before, don't go in the fields,' he said, buttering toast. 'There are crops nearing harvest in most of them. So, keep out. Also don't cross the main road at the end of the lane. Do you hear me?'

'Yes, Dad.' Paul replied.

'Peter, do you understand?' Peter nodded, he heard what his Dad said, but he didn't want to commit to anything, if he could help it. His father watched him for a moment, and then nodded himself.

'Why didn't you say okay to Dad?' Paul asked when they set off a bit later.

'I thought you'd answered for both of us. I just

agreed.' Peter walked along looking for a stick. Today he wanted a cutlass. As usual, Paul had the satchel with their dinner in. Peter's hands had to be free to deal with whatever befell them.

They crossed the lane in silence and started up a slight incline. A copse of trees shrouded the top of the hill. Reaching there they looked back, the house already looked tiny. Their mother was in the garden, hanging out some washing. Paul shouted and waved. She looked up and saw them as two dots, almost lost in the shadow of the trees. She waved back, before going indoors.

They walked through the copse and on to the top of the slope. There, they found a barbed wire fence, the rusty strands strung between old wooden posts. The path followed the fence line, and started downhill. They hadn't walked far, when they saw the reason for the fence.

Below lay an old disused slate quarry, cut back into the hill, some 150 feet high. At the bottom a derelict wooden building stood at the head of an old single track railway line. A stream bubbled down from another slope away to their left.

'Come on, let's explore.' Peter raced off. He had already forgotten his search for a stick. Paul followed his brother down the path, that levelled out at the bottom, before turning at right angles across the quarry floor.

By the time he had got down, Peter was nowhere to be seen. Paul thought that he must be in the old building and headed over that way. Before he got there, Peter popped up from behind some low scrub. 'Look at this.'

They stood together, looking at a huge cluster of toadstools growing on a dead tree. 'That must have come from up there,' Paul said, looking at the top of the quarry. He felt giddy, the clouds seemed to spill over the top.

For an hour or so they explored, at first together then separately. Paul tired of the cold, grey quarry, and went along the railway line until he reached the stream. Small fish darted about; water boatmen skidded across the surface. He sat watching a dragonfly hover and dart between the reeds. After a while he rose, and turned back towards the quarry. Dinner time, he thought.

Peter wasn't to be seen. Paul called to him, his voice echoed round the curved wall. No reply. Paul knew he wouldn't have gone home without lunch. Peter loved 'eating out'. Paul put the bag down and started looking for his brother.

'Peter, come on, where are you? Stop messing about.' Paul decided, Peter was hiding, trying to worry him. Two can play that game. Returning to the bag, he sat down, and started lunch. 'If you don't want to eat, that's up to you,'

Ten minutes, and two sandwiches later, Paul was certain his brother was out of sight and hearing. Peter wouldn't let him start eating on his own. 'No chance!'

Paul started to worry. He didn't mind his own company, but he would rather known where his brother was. There would be such a fuss, if they didn't go home together. He began searching, starting at the fallen tree where he had last seen Peter. He worked away from the railway, he hadn't seen Peter when he was down by the stream. There were cracks and crevasses everywhere that he might have hidden in. However, Paul became more and more sure, that for some reason Peter had gone home. Finally, he looked at the old building, and decided to check it. He didn't think Peter was in there, he would have been able to hear and see Paul eating.

It looked like a place where the quarry workers had come for their breaks. The hard earth floor was dry, except under holes in the roof. An old bench was fastened to one wall, the opposite wall was mostly gone. Bushes concealed what looked like a path, beside which was a raised manhole cover. Paul thought, 'you've gone down there, eh!' He crossed the shack, and looked down into inky blackness. There where footholds made of metal, going down into the darkness, but of Peter neither sight nor sound.

'Peter, are you down there?' he called. No reply. 'I'll eat your lunch.'

He decided against going down the hole: too frightening. Peter must have gone home, although for the life of him, Paul couldn't think why. He pushed the manhole cover, and was surprised when it moved. It shut down with a dull thump, dragging the undergrowth that had concealed it back into place.

Paul waited a moment to see if Peter called out. Nothing. He gathered the bag and walked home slowly. Later he was angry that he was blamed for his brother's disappearance. How it was his fault that no-one started searching until well after dark.

In fact they were all guilty of assumption. Mrs. Wilson heard Paul go into the downstairs toilet, and assumed they were both back. When he turned into the drive, Mr. Wilson saw Paul down by the chicken run. On hearing from his wife how quiet it had been, with the boy's off playing all day, he assumed they were both down by the chicken run. Paul stayed out of the way, putting off for as long as possible the moment when he would be asked where his brother was. But, as time went by Paul began to worry too. Peter had obviously gone off somewhere, but he should have got home by now.

Of course when they were called in for tea, it all came out. He would never forget the looks on his parents faces as they realised what had happened. 'Why didn't you mention it when you got home Paul?' 'Why didn't you ask if Peter was here?' 'Why didn't you say that you hadn't seen him for hours?' The questions were endless.

'I thought we were playing a game, and he was hiding from me. You know what he is like when we are playing hide and seek, he never comes out if I don't find him.' That was the best Paul could manage. The longer he put off telling about the quarry and shack, the harder it was for him to tell it at all. Finally, he told the nearest to the truth that he ever would to a police sergeant, who sat on his bed and asked about the walk.

'So you waved to your Mum. Where did you go then?'

'We went on a bit, by a quarry.'

'That must be Stammer's Pit,' said the policeman, 'did you go down there?'

' Down the path to a river, and watched the fishes.'

'And then what?'

'Ate lunch, then explored some more.' Paul didn't mention that he had eaten alone, the policeman didn't ask.

'After lunch, what did you do then?'

'I thought he was playing 'hide and seek'. We always play that. When I couldn't find him, I came home.'

'Why did you leave him there, on his own?'

Paul felt threatened by the question, and began to cry. 'I didn't leave him on his own,' he sobbed, 'I thought he'd left me – he does that all the time. He's got to be the boss of everything. I thought that he had gone home.'

'Alright Paul. That'll do for now. Wipe your tears, there's a good lad.' The policeman smiled at him, Paul felt better that he had told someone at least part of the story. He didn't want to say more to the sergeant. Peter hadn't answered when he had called. No, Paul thought, he's wondered off somewhere, got lost and the police will find him soon.

They didn't find Peter in spite of a thorough search of the whole area, there was no sign of the boy. Paul, committed to a lie, chose not to change his story. No-one noticed the manhole cover hidden in the undergrowth, behind the shack, probably because the place was so uncluttered. Anyone looking in could see that the place was empty. By the following morning, the police started to consider abduction. It was the most likely conclusion, given the facts as they were known.

As hours became days, then weeks without a sign of Peter, Paul wondered whether he should mention the manhole. If he was down there, then he has dead by now, he thought. He was surprised that he didn't mind much. Since Peter's disappearance he was the centre of his parents world. Paul grew to like the attention. After a month he didn't miss Peter at all, life was better without him.

Now, fifty years later, he had come to put the whole thing to rest. He sat in the sunshine on the large slate rock for twenty minutes or more, thinking over the events of that day years ago. Both his parents were dead, as was his own wife Clarissa, a victim of cancer, some five years before. The insurance and inheritance money from all three, enabled him to travel widely. He had only returned from abroad last week. He sighed heavily and opened a back-pack he had brought with him. Inside was a 35mm. camera, with a 1000 mm. lens and a battery powered halogen lamp. He entered the shack, it was unchanged. He was surprised that no-one had developed the site.

He found the manhole cover with difficulty, buried as it was in the vegetation. It came up slowly, creaking in protest at being disturbed. It wouldn't go completely vertical, it was too rusty. Laying flat on his stomach, he turned his attention to the shaft, shining the light down. The toe holds went down a little way and then nothing, for what looked like fifty feet or more. The bottom was visible and so he set the lamp to shine down the hole and used the camera like binoculars.

As soon as everything swam into focus, Paul saw Peter's bones. They lay where they had fallen. He looked at his brother's remains for several moments, feeling little remorse. Deep down inside, he had always known Peter was down there. He pictured him finding the manhole, seeing the toe holds, fearlessly starting down. Then, no more steps. Peter must have felt for one and lost his balance. The fall would've killed him instantly, thought Paul.

He started to get up. His right arm jarred the manhole cover, and much more easily than it had opened, it sprang shut, striking him on the head, then trapping him. Fifty years after his brother, Paul died alone in the old shaft. He was found a week later by walkers, sheltering from a shower. They saw his legs sticking out from the manhole. Thanks to his brother Paul's help, so was Peter.

Fly away Peter, fly away Paul,
Come back Peter, Come back Paul.

Doing the Right Thing

Gladys Piper looked up at the contents of her local supermarket chill cabinet. She was trying to decide what she fancied for Sunday lunch. For the rest of the week, she ate to keep body and soul alive. Sunday lunch though, now that was different.

While her husband Mickey was alive, they had always made the effort; sitting down at their dining room table, with the best linen and crockery out. She would cook a roast or something else nice, and make a pudding. Now, having been on her own for the last two years, she had maintained the tradition, but to save on heat, she sat in the lounge with a tray on her lap.

She picked up a pasta based ready meal and read the contents details. No faddy diet for her, she was just watching fat and salt intake. Gladys didn't have any weight problems and was still trim for sixty eight. With a shrug, she returned the packet, deciding against pasta. She moved along to the fish counter.

Not needing much shopping she had picked up a basket. Bending to put it down at her feet by the counter, she saw the bit of paper. It had a familiar appearance. Gladys looked around quickly, there was no-one close by. The fish counter assistant was occupied, packing something in cling-film. Using the basket to cover her action, Gladys picked up the paper with a gloved hand.

Immediately, she knew it was money. Still no-one

was interested in her. Opening her handbag, she dropped it in. At first it looked like a twenty pound note, folded into four. Unfolding it revealed three notes. Sixty pounds!

If asked – under normal circumstances – Gladys Piper would declare that she was an honest woman. She always tried to do the right thing. Now, she picked up the shopping basket and crossed to the in-store café. There, she bought a cup of tea, and found a table to herself. Opened her handbag, she made sure that it was sixty pounds. Yes!

The fish counter was visible from her table. For the next fifteen minutes or so, she sipped tea and watched to see if anyone appeared, who might be looking for something. Nothing happened. What was she to do? A large part of her said, 'give it to the assistant.' A smaller part was making much more noise, saying 'keep it'.

In her bag, she had an envelope containing a gas bill, together with the hard saved money to pay it. Her next stop was the Post Office. Sixty pounds would come in very handy.

Whoever dropped it can't be missing it, she thought taking a deep breath. Whatever am I thinking? I cannot justify it like that. Keeping it is stealing. Besides, it might be a pensioner like me. She sat still for some time, then with a small sigh, finished her tea, and crossed back to the fish counter.

The assistant smiled at her as she approached. 'Can I help you, love?'

'Well well, look at this.' Bending down as if she had just found it, Gladys continued. 'Some folk, I don't know.' Holding up the money she said, 'Looks like some people have money to throw away.'

The assistant looked at the notes 'Was it down there on the floor?'

'Yes, by the counter.'

'How much is there?'

Appearing to check as if she didn't know, Gladys replied 'sixty pounds. Shall I take it over to customer service?' Gladys was beginning to feel better about her decision.

'It's all right love,' the assistant came around the counter, 'I'll see to it for you.' Gladys said nothing as she handed over the money. 'It's good of you to do this,' the girl said, 'not many would've I can tell you. Now then dear, did you want some fish?'

Gladys bought a salmon steak, and went to pay for her shopping. The fish counter assistant watched her pass through the checkout. Silly old bat she thought, why hand the money in? Should have kept it, I'm going to; it's my Saturday night out paid for. Who's going to know?

She went behind the screen at the back of the counter, opened the top button of her overall, and pushed the notes down into her bra, shivering slightly as the cold paper touched her skin.

Gladys walked towards the post office. Whilst she was feeling very good about having done the right thing, there was still a part of her that bemoaned a lost opportunity. Standing in the queue at the Post Office, she took the envelope with her gas bill, together with the money to pay it, from her handbag. As she did, she became aware of a conversation going on at the counter.

'I'm very sorry, dear. Nothing has been handed in.'

'I've dropped it somewhere, I'd hoped it was here.'

'Have you been anywhere else?'

'Only the supermarket.'

Gladys watched a young girl with a baby in a pushchair, go out into the street. Several minutes later, gas bill paid, she followed. The girl was outside, adjusting the baby's coat.

Gladys went to her, 'Excuse me, I couldn't help overhearing in there. Have you lost some money?' Her concern for the girl stopped her thinking clearly. It all seemed so fortunate, finding the person who had lost the money.

The young girl looked quietly at her for a moment, then nodded. 'Yes, why, have you found any?'

'Yes, I did.' Gladys was so pleased her honesty had been rewarded, that she hugged the girl, then blurted out, 'it was sixty pounds, wasn't it?'

Pulling away slightly embarrassed, the girl responded more quickly wit a nod. 'Oh! Thank you, I didn't know what I was going to do. I'm on my own, see.'

'I found it on the floor in the supermarket and handed it in.' Gladys said. 'Come on, I'll take you.' They went back together, along the road. By the time they had reached the store, Gladys had learnt that the girl was called Annabel, and the baby Tommy.

A supervisor was standing just inside the entrance. After hearing what Gladys had to say, she asked them to wait while she went over to the fish-counter. She returned a few moments later, saying that the assistant was claiming that she knew nothing about any money being handed in.

'You'd better come over, ma'am,' she said to Gladys. 'We can check that it's the same girl.' When she saw Gladys, the fish counter assistant blushed.

'That's the girl that served me,' Gladys told the supervisor, 'and the one I gave the sixty pounds to'.

The supervisor took the assistant behind the stand,

and a couple of minutes later, reappeared with the money. 'Get your things,' she told the assistant, 'and report to the office.'

She handed the money to Gladys with an apology. When they got outside the store, Gladys gave Annabel the sixty pounds.

'Thank you so much,' the youngster said. 'Goodness knows what we would have done, if you hadn't found it. Not everyone would have handed it in.' With more grateful thanks from Annabel, they went their separate ways.

Gladys smiled to herself. Now she was feeling really good, more certain than ever that she had done the right thing.

Annabel and her baby brother, went in through their front door. 'We're back Mum.' She walked through into the kitchen, where an older woman was sitting at the table with a mug of coffee and a newspaper. 'You'll never guess what happened. We lost Tommy's favourite toy car, that Aunty May sent him.' The older woman looked up, about to say something.

Before she could speak, Annabel continued. 'I was asking about it at the Post Office, when this old women thought I'd lost some money. Apparently, she had found it at the supermarket, and would you believe it, she handed it in. Instead of asking me to say how much I had lost, she was stupid enough to tell me what she had found.'

While she was speaking, Annabel had taken Tommy out of his pushchair. 'We went back to the supermarket. The old biddy told them it was mine. So they gave it to her, and she gave it to me – forty quid, good or what? I'll split it fifty-fifty with you.' Smiling to herself, Annabel handed her mother one of the notes.

The Dogmatic Philosopher

It was just a normal day in the square. Normal that was, until about twenty five to four, when the dog first appeared.

Brian Harrison, denizen of the town's main square – in daylight hours at least – spotted it, as he sat on what was commonly known as Brian's Bench. Protected on the one side by the canopy of a large oak tree and on the other by a bus shelter, it provided him with an adequately weatherproof, daytime 'office'.

It would be far too simplistic a thing, to define Brian as a layabout, drop-out or any other kind of 'out'. He was essentially a city centre philosopher, who held court daily on this bench. Occasionally, people passing by would pause for a word, a few would sit for a while. They may smoke cigarettes together, though never Brian's. His favourite brand was other people's. Now and again, someone would bring him a plastic cup of tea from the burger bar across the square.

Most of the town's population knew of him, even if they didn't actually know him to speak to. Generally, he wore an old Army greatcoat over jeans, a tee shirt and very well-worn boots. His long, light coloured hair was shaved back on either side of his head, leaving the top stretching hedge-like, from his forehead to well below his collar. The most striking thing about him though, was his steely, blue grey eyes. If he fixed you with them, it was nearly impossible to turn away.

He didn't have any friends *per se*. Not the real 'support you through thick and thin' type of friends. Everyone thought that they knew Brian, but his built in defence mechanism let no-one into his life after dark. Where he went and what he did when he left the square, was something that he kept very much to himself. Mind, by the same token, no-one seemed that interested.

The dog was a black and brown, short-haired terrier. It probably could – most charitably – be described as a mongrel. Brian hadn't seen precisely where it came from. Suddenly it was there, standing in front of him, looking up into his eyes.

'Hello dog, who do you belong to?' Almost before he had asked the question, Brian felt that he knew the answer. 'Homeless eh!'

The dog moved closer, Brian was able to reach down and ruffle it's ears. Under the bench stood a couple of plastic cups half full of cold tea. Consolidating them into one, he lent forwards holding it while the dog lapped eagerly.

'So you were thirsty, eh? Hungry as well I bet.' Brian felt that he was right in that assumption, without being quite sure why. He looked around, trying to see a familiar face, but to no avail. With a sigh he got up, clicked his fingers and headed for the burger bar. The dog followed. Somehow, Brian knew that it would.

He bought a burger and they returned to the seat. The dog sat at his feet and watched the food being broken into bite sized pieces. Brian lent forward, offering the first piece. 'Careful, it's hot,' he said.

The dog took it gingerly, champed at it for a moment, then with a lick of the tongue that went right round his mouth, it was gone. Brian gave him the next piece. When the burger had all gone, Brian looked down at the dog. 'Right, so you've had a drink and some food, now I suppose you'll be off.'

The dog rose from where he had sat to eat. He walked slowly underneath the bench, turned and lay down, resting his head on his front paws. Looking down, Brian saw the dog's eyes watching him.

'What's your name, or is that something else you want me to give you?' Brian felt silly the moment he had said it. Talking to a dog was just about all right, most people did that. Expecting answers was another thing. But, he was quite certain, the dog had told him that his name was Danny. Not 'told him' in the spoken sense, rather he had inclined Brian to believe that he'd been told.

They held each other's gaze for several moments. Finally, Brian looked away and sat perfectly still, deep in thought. Then he glanced up at the church tower clock. Just after four fifteen. A bit earlier than usual, but never mind, he had things to do.

Standing up, he gathered empty cups and other rubbish from around the bench, then set off along the pavement. Danny followed some ten feet behind. Brian dropped the litter into a waste bin and without a backward glance, started out towards home.

He lived with his mother. It worked well for both of them. She had some company, he got his laundry done and a hot meal each evening. They shared the household running costs. What would happen to his street credibility if it became common knowledge, he didn't worry about. Up until now, it had never been an issue. The dog would be their first 'visitor' for a long time. Brian smelt onions frying as he walked in through the front door.

'Home Mum,' his usual greeting. 'What's for tea?'

'Liver.' The voice came through a closed door that led to the kitchen. 'Who's that with you?' Brian looked down at the dog and then at the closed door. How the heck did she know?

'Danny,' he said, waiting to see what response that would get.

'Whatever do you want with a dog?'

She must have seen them coming, Brian thought. Then he remembered, she'd not used the front door in the three years since dad had died. She always used the back door. He removed and hung up his coat and went through into the kitchen. His mother was standing at the stove frying liver. She glanced back at them both.

'Get an old blanket out of the airing cupboard, there's a good lad. Put it in the lounge by the fire place. He can sleep there on it.'

Brian looked at his mother. She was reacting to Danny in much the same way that he had. It was as if she knew him already. He went upstairs as he'd been told too. Coming down with the blanket, he heard his mother's voice.

'Sorry Mum,' he said as he re-entered the kitchen. 'Did you say something?'

'I was just talking to Danny.'

Brian looked at her, and smiled. 'Mother, will you listen to yourself? Talking to a dog.' As he spoke, he looked down at Danny. 'Oh, I know I talk to you as well. That is a bit different though. I actually know you.'

'How?' said his mother. 'You only met him an hour ago.'

'You cannot possibly know that.' Brian felt that he was losing control of the whole situation. What's more, he was sure that the dog knew it too.

'Yes I can Brian, Danny told me. Also, he said he would prefer a cheese burger next time.'

Brian sat down in a state of shock. Things had been rather strange at the square, when he'd felt that Danny was in some way communicating with him. But his mother was acting as if the two of them were old friends.

'You'll have to eat what we are having tonight Danny,' she went on. 'I'll get you some proper dog food tomorrow. Which one do you like?'

That was absolutely too much for Brian. 'Now stop it mother. This joke has gone on quite long enough.'

'He likes tinned dog food,' Mrs. Harvester said with a knowing smile in her eyes, 'but he prefers those little dry things they show on the TV.'

'Are you telling me now that he watches television?' Brian looked at her in amazement.

'Don't be silly, Brian. Now then, have you washed your hands? I'm about ready to serve up.' The three of them ate in silence. Brian and his mother sat at the kitchen table, where they usually had their meals. Danny ate his from a bowl on the floor beside the sink. He didn't wolf at the food, in the way that dogs usually did. Rather he took his time, as if he was savouring every mouthful.

Deep in his own thoughts, Brian watched the dog eating. What was going on here? His mother had never been that fond of dogs, yet she had taken to Danny. Worse, he was settling in quite happily. This must end, thought Brian. He was in full control of his life, every aspect of it. There was absolutely no room for anyone else. That included a smart dog.

Finally he broke the silence. 'I'll take him down to the RSPCA in the morning,' he said, watching the dog while he spoke.

'Why?' said his mother, a little too indignantly for Brian's liking. 'He can stay here with us?'

'Someone may be looking for him, may be worried about him.' Somehow, Brian knew that he was clutching at straws.

'Not around here, you can be certain about that, Brian.' Mrs Harvester rose from the table and took the empty plates to the sink. She bent down to pick up Danny's bowl.

'You don't know that mother. How on earth could you?' As he spoke, Brian realised his foolishness. 'Of course, don't tell me. Danny told you.'

His mother nodded, at the same time starting to wash the dishes. 'It's really quite a sad story. He was travelling with some people from up north. They stopped at the Motorway Services and let him out for a run. When he got back, the car had gone.'

'Ask him their name. He does names. We could try to contact them, tell them where he is.'

'He doesn't want to go back to them, Brian.' Dishes clattered onto the drainer. 'Would you? Let's face it, they didn't take very good care of him.'

Brian looked down at Danny. He sat close to Mrs. Harvester's legs, looking back up at him.

'That's right is it?' Brian asked. 'You want to stay here with us?'

They only held eye contact for a moment, but in that time he learnt just how the dog felt. Brian was overwhelmed by the clarity of Danny's thoughts. However, it did need them to be able to see each other, make some kind of eye contact. Mother is in touch with this animal through closed doors, he thought.

The following morning, he got ready to leave for the square. Opening the front door, Brian called out to

Danny. The dog padded through beside Mrs. Harvester and they stood together. She was out on the front step, for the first time in years. Brian stood by the gate and called to Danny again. The dog sat down, he wasn't going to move.

'Think you must have frightened him last night, with your talk of the RSPCA,' his mother said.

'He can't stay here all day with you.' Brian knew he had already lost the moral high ground. 'What are you both going to do?'

'I am quite sure we will find plenty to talk about,' said Mrs. Harvester. 'See you this evening Brian.' She quietly shut the front door.

Brian was lost in thought as he walked towards the city centre. For the first time in his life, he was at a total loss. Brian Harvester, the man with an opinion about everything and an answer for most. Beaten by a stray dog!

His day turned out to be fairly routine. He saw a few people he knew and chatted with a several others. He drank a couple of plastic cups of tea and smoked several cigarettes. The sun shone for most of the day; he was able to remove his greatcoat in the afternoon.

It was just a normal day in the square. Normal that was, until about twenty five to four, when the cat first appeared.

The Red Scarf

A ferocious storm swept the coast that Sunday afternoon. When Jane Temple first saw the object, she couldn't make it out. Something soft, fluttering in the gale, two hundred yards away along the deserted promenade. Leaning into the wind, she walked closer. She saw it was soft and red, maybe an item of clothing. She put her foot on it, then bent down, picking it up with two fingers. A hand knitted scarf; very nice in spite of being sodden.

Jane placed it flat on the sea wall. A name tag read 'A E Jackman.' Obviously valued, its owner clearly didn't want to lose it; or was it a child's? She picked it up, squeezed the water out as best she could. Then, folding it up, she set off home.

Twenty minutes later, with a hot cup of coffee warming her hands, she looked at the scarf, laying on her kitchen table. 'So A E Jackman,' she said aloud – something she did as she lived alone – 'who are you?' Putting her cup down, she went into the hall, to get her telephone directory.

There were three local entries for Jackman. None were A E. That's OK Jane thought, she might not be on the telephone. She had decided, the scarf's owner was undoubtedly female.

Sitting on the bottom step of the hall stairs, she dialled the first number. B. Jackman was an elderly lady;

she apologised, unable to help. The next, a retired Naval Commander Malcolm P, checked with his wife first, then said that they didn't know an A E Jackman. There was no reply to the third number. That's the one Jane thought, then realised she was thinking illogically. Still, she noted the address down.

The following morning, Jane went to her local library to search the Electoral Register. She took a flask of coffee and some biscuits. Since accepting early retirement a year ago, she'd lacked direction. Several different evening courses hadn't help her find her niche. Trivial though it may be, Jane wanted A E Jackman to have her scarf back.

First she found the address for the unanswered call. FR, and WN Jackman, so no help there. Bother she thought, I'll have to start from the beginning. Two hours, three cups of coffee and five ginger snaps later, she had her first possible. There was an A Jackman at 8 Hewitts Terrace. That's bed-sit land, she thought. Four surnames in one house, these will be students. She made a note on her pad, and continued searching.

When she finally found A E Jackman, she was amazed. Andrea Ellen had reached her eighteenth birthday last month. The surprising bit was, that she lived with Ellen Margaret and Commander Malcolm P. Jackman Rtd. Last evening they had denied all knowledge of her. To be certain, Jane finished checking the register. No other possibility emerged.

On arriving home, she considered what her search had uncovered. Maybe the scarf belonged to a visitor to the town, or someone who hadn't registered to vote. No. The one indisputable fact was that – for whatever reason – Commander Jackman had lied to her. They must know this A E Jackman. She went into the kitchen to prepare her dinner. Since retiring, she hadn't changed her meal time. Six pm, in company with the television news.

Later, she considered what to do next. Am I making too much out of this she thought, holding the now dry scarf in her hands? The label was similar to the type, used to mark school uniforms. Andrea Ellen Jackman might have had some left from her schooldays, and so marked this valued scarf. Just eighteen, maybe she was off to University, and so marked all her clothes. Whatever, Jane wanted her to have it back.

Why had the Commander – almost certainly her father – denied all knowledge of her. 'No, that's not quite true,' Jane said aloud, 'I asked if he knew an A E Jackman. I'd no idea of her name, or sex then.' She decided he would have realised.

'What secret aren't you telling me?' She smiled to herself, she was talking to a scarf.

By Tuesday breakfast, she had made up her mind upon a plan of action. She was going to visit the Jackmans to return the scarf, and that would be that. The storm had nearly abated. It was mild for a February morning. She dressed for outdoors, putting the scarf in a paper bag.

The Jackman home was about a mile away. The Navy must pay well, Jane thought as she walked up the drive of a 1930s detached house. A pleasant looking, middle aged woman answered the door bell.

'Hello,' Jane smiled, 'Mrs. Jackman?' The woman nodded. Jane continued quickly, 'I am so sorry to bother you, but I think that this might be yours.' She took the scarf out of the bag. Before she could hand it over, a voice sounded from within. 'Who is it, dear?' A man appeared at the door, and looked firstly at Jane, and then at the scarf. Neither of them showed any indication, that they recognised it. Mrs. Jackman stepped back, leaving her husband to face Jane.

She explained about finding the scarf, seeing that it was labelled and tracking it to this house. 'Are you the person who rang us last night?' Jackman asked. When Jane nodded, he continued. 'I told you then, we do not know anyone with those initials. I am sorry, but we can't help.'

He moved back inside the door. Jane told them about the entry in the electoral register. They looked at each other for a second or two; she thought that Mrs. Jackman had flushed slightly. Jackman spoke quietly. 'I can't explain how that's happened. It's quite obviously a mistake. They do make mistakes sometimes you know.' The front door closed. Jane walked home.

Now what she thought? I could hand it in to the police, tell them about the Jackmans and let them sort it out. Would they bother with lost property? Probably not. She decided that there was one other course of action. Instead of going straight home, she walked down onto the promenade. It took just a few moments to reach the spot where, two days earlier, she had picked up the scarf.

She looked both ways; to the right, the promenade stretched away for more than a mile; to the left, fifty yards from where she stood, the road turned left, up into town. The footpath dropped down onto the beach. Jane walked that way, in the direction the scarf had come from.

In a moment she was walking on the sand. For the first time since she had found the scarf, Jane felt she was being drawn forwards. She walked towards a rocky outcrop at the base of the cliff, thirty yards further on.

Rounding it, she saw the beach curve away ahead. She carried on along the tide line. 'What am I looking for?' she said aloud. The sea was still quite rough. She felt the misty spray; tasting salt on her lips. She moved up the beach towards the cliff, located a suitable rock and sat down. She watched the breakers for several minutes, then looked back along the base of the cliff, in the direction from where she had just come.

At first she saw a shoe that she thought might have been left by the tide. 'No, it's to far above the high water mark.' Again she spoke out loud. Getting up from her seat on the rock, she walked back slowly towards the shoe. As she reached it, she was horrified to see that it was on a foot. A little to one side, half covered with the sand and scree, was another foot, this time shoeless. Both feet were protruding from a small mound, that had obviously been disturbed by the weekend storm.

Jane was sure she was looking at a concealed body. The shoe obviously belonged to a woman. Jane was in no doubt, that it was Andrea Ellen Jackman lying here. Now, it would be up to the police, to discover exactly why.

The Final Answer

Carol Wakefield curled up on the sofa, sipping red wine. She was watching her husband Dave take part in a television quiz show. Within easy reach on a coffee table was the open bottle of wine, some Belgian chocolates, and her mobile phone.

Carol was absolutely certain of the precise moment she had fallen in love with Dave. She'd been celebrating her nineteenth birthday, with her best friend Beryl and some of the girls from work. They'd met up at a local pub, before going on to a Chinese Restaurant. Several bottles of wine with the food, helped them enjoy a good evening. After, they went on to a club.

Dave was there when they arrived, standing at the bar with some mates. Carol spotted him straight away. She manoeuvred her group close to the group of boys. 'I'll get this round' she said, turning to the bar. They were side by side. She started ordering drinks.

Dave had watched her with a slight smile, until she faced him.

'What?' Carol said, churning inside.

'Nothing–' Dave looked at the growing mass of glasses. 'Having a party?'

'Yeh! My round–.' Carol was loosing control, and not because of alcohol.

'Let me pay.' He reached for his wallet.

'No, I couldn't, anyway it's my birthday.' The minute she'd spoken, Carol wished she hadn't. Now he knew something about her. She didn't even know his name.

He read her mind, 'My name's Dave. Look, at least let me buy you a drink, for your birthday.'

'Why? You – I don't know you.' Carol wasn't doing this very well. As she paid for the drinks she'd ordered, she dropped her purse.

Dave retrieved it before she could react. Their fingers touched as he returned it. That was that.

They found a couple of tables away from the dance floor. Her friends sat at one, she and Dave the other. Beryl flitted between the two groups for a while; until a visit to the 'Ladies' gave Carol the chance, to ask her best friend for some space. 'I'm fine, promise.' Carol said. 'I'll ring you tomorrow.' Beryl rejoined the other girls on the dance floor.

They shared a taxi, he asked the driver to wait when they reached her house. 'I'll ring you?' Dave smiled at her. 'I'd like to see you again.' He didn't try to kiss her.

'Oh! alright,' Carol opened her handbag. 'I'll give you my mobile number.'

'Just dial it onto mine.' He gave her his 'phone; she tapped her number in, and he saved it .

'What's yours?' she asked softly.

'I'll ring you tomorrow. Store my number then.' He walked to the taxi.

She had hoped he would kiss her. Somehow, she wasn't disappointed when he didn't try. She was in love and didn't want to rock the boat. He was absolutely worth waiting for. She opened the front door, looking back to watch until the taxi was out of sight

Her phone woke her at nine the next morning, a Sunday. She'd put it by the bed, just in case.

'Good morning. Did I wake you?' he said quietly.

She thought he was still be in bed.

'Yes,' she breathed the words, still half asleep.

'Good. I wanted to be the first person you speak to today.'

'What about you?' she said, who have you spoken to already?'

He laughed, 'I've just this second wakened up.'

He was still in bed. She tried to imagine his body laying there, but could only see his face.

'What are you doing today?' he asked.

'Nothing much, lunch with Mum and Dad; a lazy day. You know the sort of thing.'

'Can you excuse yourself from lunch there?'

'I could, why?' She knew what was coming next.

'I'll pick you up at midday, we can go out for lunch.'

'I'll be ready." He broke the connection. She stored his number on her mobile under 'D'.

The next three months were intense. They were together all the time, occasionally with friends. It surprised no-one when they announced their intention to marry. Carol asked Beryl to be her bridesmaid.

The ceremony and reception was at the local golf club, the sun shone throughout. 'It wouldn't dare not.' Beryl said to Carol's mother. They were sharing a pot of tea, after getting Carol ready.

'How are you settling in at university?' the older woman asked.

Beryl was at Manchester studying Graphic Design. 'Oh, fine. It's a bit strange, but I'm getting there, slowly.'

The honeymoon was in Florida. There, for the first time, they made love. 'You are special to me Carol,' Dave had always said, from the start. 'I'm not sleeping with you until we're married.' Half of Carol loved him for that respect, the other, much bigger half was frustrated to hell.

The next four years flew by. They progressed well in their different careers. Carol had been promoted to day shift manager at the Call Centre, she'd joined straight from school. Dave was regional sales manager with a builders' merchants.

They had bought a house just outside town – the best of both worlds – a bit of the country life, whilst commuting daily to work. Totally content with each other, their life was good. Children were not part of the plan, for at least another three years; much to both their mothers disgust.

'Look Mum, I know you want to be a Grandmother,' Carol said, when they'd met for lunch one day, shortly after their first wedding anniversary. 'We want children, but we want financial security first.'

Three evenings a week, they'd eat dinner, watching the latest craze to sweep the nation. A television quiz in which contestants could win large sums of money, by answering general knowledge questions. They joked about Dave getting on.

'I'm sure I could answer enough to win a decent amount.' Dave said.

'Well, ring up then,' Carol said. 'You won't know unless you try.'

He'd been successful at the thirteenth attempt.

'Who said thirteen is unlucky? he said, packing an overnight case for the trip to the studio. Contestants could telephone a friend for help with one answer. He'd asked her to be one of his 'friends', together with Beryl and a colleague that he worked with. He was taking his Dad for support. She hugged and kissed him goodbye, watching him drive away.

That had been yesterday morning. Now, she

watched him answered question after question, until he had won a quarter million. She sat motionless. She heard the show's host tell him that the next question was for half a million. 'You don't have to answer it, Dave. You can walk away with a cheque for two hundred and fifty thousand pounds, right now. You can have a look at the question and walk away; you can still phone a friend. It's up to you.'

Dave nodded, taking a deep breath. The half million pound question, together with it's four alternative answers appeared on the screen.

Who was the American President throughout the first World War? The options were, William Taft, Calvin Coolidge, Woodrow Wilson or Herbert Hoover.

Carol's heart missed a beat. She knew. Wilson served two terms from 1913 to 1921; he was in office during the 1914–1918 War. She watched Dave, realising from his manner, that he either didn't know, or wasn't certain. The compere repeated the question, reminding him that he could take the £250,000, and he could still phone a friend.

'What are you thinking, Dave?' he asked.

Dave flicked his hair back from his forehead with a finger, a sure sign to Carol and to his father in the audience, that he didn't know. 'I wish I'd paid more attention to history at school,' he said. 'I had better phone a friend.'

'Who's that going to be, Dave?'

Carol picked up her mobile. 'Come on, my darling,' she thought, 'think of what half a million would mean to us. Ring me!'

Dave thought for a few seconds, looking down at his knees.

'What are you thinking, Dave?' the host asked. 'You

don't have to take their answer. You can take the cheque for £250,000. However if you give me a wrong answer, you will loose £218,000. It's up to you.'

Now Carol was shouting at the television screen. 'Ring me, Dave. I know the answer.'

He looked up at the compere, and with a sigh, said 'I'll ring Beryl.'

'Is Beryl your wife?'

'No, she's a friend."

'Will she know the answer?' the sound of a telephone ringing started.

Carol froze. 'Would Beryl know, what was Dave thinking of? Beryl was into graphic design. History wasn't her thing. Why hadn't he rung me?'

Her mind was numb. She heard Beryl answer the phone. The compere told her the position, and then Dave read Beryl the question.

There followed a pause of no more than a couple of seconds, that seemed like eternity to Carol. Then Beryl said, 'I think it was Taft, Dave.'

How sure are you Beryl?' Dave asked. A clock that was counting down the thirty seconds allowed for the call. 'You have ten seconds.'

Beryl thought for three of them, 'Ninety percent sure Dave.'

'Ok, Beryl. Thanks.' Dave looked up above his head.

'You don't have to play Dave. You can take the quarter million. You know that.' The host spoke quietly. Dave nodded.

Carol was on her mobile ringing Beryl.

'Hi Carol.' Caller identification on her phone, told Beryl who was ringing

'Why did you say Taft if you weren't sure? Why didn't you say you didn't know?' Carol was crying, the words coming between sobs.

Beryl said, 'Carol, I thought it was right, I promise you. Isn't it?'

'No, Beryl. It most certainly isn't. It was Wilson. Are you watching?'

'I wasn't, but after the phone call I put it straight on. I am watching now. Surely, he'll take the money if he isn't sure.'

'I don't know what he'll do, Beryl. I thought I knew him, but that was before he rang you for a history question. Now, who knows what he will do.

The lifelong friends sat a couple of miles apart, linked by their mobile phones, watching the television.

'What do you want to do, Dave?'

He looked across at the compere who had now become his tormentor.

'I want to play. I'll never get a better chance at half a million pounds, but–.'

'Ninety percent is quite high, Dave. Beryl seemed fairly sure. What does she do for a living?'

'She's doing a degree in graphic design.' Dave replied, instantly feeling a little silly, for ringing her with this question.

'Is she any good at history?' The compere smiled. 'Don't answer that Dave; it's up to you, you can leave now with a cheque for £250,000. You don't have to answer this question. If you get it wrong, you'd lose a lot of money. It's up to you.'

Carol watched her husband, she'd stopped crying now. He was going to answer, and he would be wrong. Alright, he'd won £32,000. That was nice. If he had rung her, they would have been up half a million.

'Carol,' Beryl was talking on the mobile.

'Yeh.'

'I'm so sorry, I really thought it was Taft. I wouldn't have said it, if I hadn't been sure.'

'Beryl, I'm not angry with you. It's Dave. Why did he think you'd know that? Just because you're at university.'

They watched the tableau unfold in the television studio. The lights, the music, the two men sitting at the console in the middle of the screen. One confident and comfortable in his success, the other tormented by the choice he knew he had to make.

I'm going to play,' Dave had squared up in the seat, now that he had made up his mind. 'I am going with Beryl's answer. It's Taft,' he said firmly and clearly. 'Final answer.'

Disappearing Summer

The noise of the battle was unimaginable, the air full of acrid smoke from exploding shells. It had been raging on and off for a couple of hours, going on five years; or so it appeared to most of the young soldiers, as they watched events unfold. Time for them seemed to stand still. Some looked on with interest, some in abject fear. Others sat with their backs to the action, trying to block out the certainty that soon, they too would have to go down onto the battlefield.

Two hundred and fifty men sat in groups, under the shelter of the tree covered slope on that summer day in 1916. Below them, a field bathed in warm sunshine stretched down to a river, and to a bridge that spanned it. That was the objective; both sides needed the crossing. The extent of that need was made obvious, by the large numbers of bodies already lying across the field. The main force had dug in, this side of the river, fifty yards from the bridge. The resting men on the slope were being held in reserve.

Soon, they would be ordered to cross the field, to act as a distraction from the main offensive on the bridge. The officers who had made that decision sat at tables covered with maps, papers, hats and gloves in a bunker, two miles behind the front line. To them, the field was an irregular green shape on the map; the strategically vital bridge just two parallel lines half an inch long.

David Wilkinson and Terry Black sat together,

smoking. Both twenty years old, they were from very different walks of life. Terry's father was a miner who had lost his right leg in a pit accident. James Black hadn't wanted his son to go down the pit. When the Army Recruiting Unit had come to their village, Terry had joined. His mother had cried every single day since he'd left, her letters were often tear stained. He had struck up an instant friendship with David Wilkinson, in spite of their differences. Terry, a half educated beer drinker, liked listening to his new public school friend talk, as much for how as for what he said.

David was happily drawn to Terry. He valued the friendship, in stark contrast to his more usual, advantaged acquaintances. He'd volunteered too, much against his parents wishes. His defiance was due entirely to his father telling everyone that he lacked moral fibre. The evening that David told his parents, his mother shut her husband out of their bedroom. 'It stays like that, until David returns, safe and well,' she said.

Her letters wrote of shortages, the problems of estate management with everyone away. They had opened the stables as a Medical Centre for wounded, who were already returning home.

Rugby united the two young men. During basic training, they'd played together at the heart of the pack. They would probably have played for the Army, but for the war.

The two friends watched a lone figure coming down through the trees. 'Despatches,' said David, squinting to see through the smoke. 'Bet we're going in'. Terry said. The more experienced men had already gone forward. It must be their turn to show what they could do. Minutes later it was confirmed, 'kick-off' three pm. Just thirty minutes to go.

They looked at each other, and began checking their rifles. Neither spoke, they had nothing to say. The bravado that had brought them this far must now be accounted too. The minutes passed quickly. They listened with their colleagues to the final briefing. The task was to cross the field in skirmishing fashion, making noise and drawing enemy fire. If and when they reached the forward position, down by the river, they could take cover. The force making the main attack on the bridge needed a few moments to cross the open ground, in front of those forward trenches.

The young Captain relaying the orders, was as inexperienced as his men. 'Our job is to give them that time, lads'. His lack of enthusiasm failed to impart confidence in the men that he led. 'Wait for my whistled signal, then good luck to you all,' was the best he could manage.

Terry and David shook hands. 'See you in the trenches.' Terry smiled as he spoke. David thought how white his friends' teeth were. 'Yes. Look after yourself.' He spoke with emotion shallow in his throat. It would be easy for him to break down, but that would vindicate his father's belief. He glanced along the line, everybody looked much the same. Could we do this, he wondered?

The whistle sounded. With a roar, they left the safety of the trees, moving down onto the field. The enemy might just as well have blown the whistle; they were ready and waiting. Before the reserve group had left the tree-line, the ground erupted a few yards ahead. Some stopped in their tracks in shock. Others fell, slashed by shrapnel, earth and stones. The young Captain was thrown in the air like a rag doll. Some of those still rushing forward, passed under his flailing body.

When the second salvo arrived, most of them were

crossing the target area. The shells wrought more death and injury, despite landing behind the main advance. David ran, sometimes stumbling on the uneven ground. He trod on a body, lurched, then fell beside it. Stay down, stay here, his mind screamed at him. He got up quickly, running on into the smoke, firing his rifle into the air so as not to hit any of his colleagues. He saw Terry away to one side, running, shooting, grinning. What can he possibly find to laugh about? David thought. He veered towards his friend.

He had almost caught up with him, when the enemy artillery, several hundred yards beyond the river fired again. David had passed Terry, before he realised his friend had stopped. He look to see that all was well, but Terry was on his knees, his hands clutching at his stomach, screaming soundlessly. No-one stopped David from going back. He caught his friend by his shoulders, then laid him gently down onto the grass; kneeling to look at the extent of his injuries. The tall grass hid them.

He tried to move Terry's hands but couldn't. He was holding onto his stomach, which had been torn open by pieces of shrapnel. There was blood on the grass where he now lay. He was as good as dead. David felt his tears well up. He stood to see if there was a medic anywhere in sight.

A sniper, high in a church tower beyond the river, had seen the two men go down in the grass. When they first stopped running, he shot at them, but missed. He waited and his patience was rewarded, when one man stood up. He squeezed off a shot.

David barely felt the soft nosed bullet. It entered his back just below his left shoulder-blade, smashed through bone and soft tissue, before continuing downwards, through his left lung. It exited making a large hole in his chest. He was thrown back by the impact, across the lifeless mess that had been Terry. He lost consciousness, and their blood mixed.

Just a moment passed, then David came to. He felt very cold, movement was difficult. The noise of the battle seemed distant. He could feel the sun, but it didn't warm him. 'You all right, Terry?' He just managed to speak through chattering teeth. Terry didn't respond. David looked to see why he couldn't move. His chest and Terry's stomach seemed to be joined. He slipped back into unconsciousness.

He was home again, riding through the north side of the family estate. The sun was warm, the harvest could only be days away. The fields were yellow, waiting for the sun to burnish them to gold. High in the sky, a kestrel hunted along the line of the hedge, hovering with its head motionless, waiting for the first sign of prey on the ground beneath.

He came awake again, this time he knew he was dying. His breath bubbled in his chest, his shattered lung losing its fight to breathe. He was drowning in his own blood. He looked down at Terry, and wept tears for them both.

He felt warm tears rolling down his cheeks, as he knelt holding the big canine head in his arms. Even in death, the red setter's coat shone. Eight years old, was far too young to cope with the death of a best friend. They had always been together. He was ten years younger than this dog; he had not known life without him. In the warmth of the summer sunshine, he looked across to his father, who was digging a grave, under the big yew tree behind the main stable block.

Maybe, if I could stand up, I might attract some help for Terry, he thought. He was trying to move, but his ability to do so was gone. In fact he was barely alive, as he slipped into unconsciousness again.

He lay on his back in the warm, sun dappled shade, beneath one of the old oaks that lined the drive. The sky was blue, but for the occasional lost cloud. School was over, all that was left was the wait for his exam results. Should be all right, he had worked hard enough, Didn't want to go to University though. Much rather go to Agricultural College, learn how to run this place properly. One day the farm would all be his.

'David'. His mother called.

He looked at his watch, tea time. 'Coming, mother', he called. Getting slowly to his feet, he crossed the drive and went into the front door.

Their bodies were recovered later that evening, and laid side by side. One hundred and nine young men died that afternoon. The bridge wasn't taken that day, nor for another two months. The enemy just retreated one dark night, leaving it to the final victors. Much later, the autumn rain would wash away the blood, from the field of summer death.

In at the Deep End

If asked, I would probably say that I first meet Jack Davies a week ago. But after second thoughts, it's possibly nearer a month. Damn it; how time flies when you're the wrong side of fifty.

A mutual friend had put us together. I happened to mention that my wife Becky and I, wanted to invest in some decent art and furniture for the house we'd just purchased.

'You know Jack Davies?' the friend asked.

'No,' I replied, 'should I?'

With a noncommittal shrug, he said, 'I'll put you in touch.'

'Why? What does he do?' I decided to show interest.

'It's easier to say what he doesn't do.'

I decided to leave it at that, and a couple of days later he rang me.

'Hi. This is Jack Davies. I understand you need my help.'

We arranged to meet at our local pub that evening. I arrived early, seeking 'home turf' advantage. He was already there. We shook hands and he paid for two pints of real ale. We found a table in a quite corner.

He turned out to be the kind of guy it's good to know. He'd probably lived his forty five or so years to the full. Small at five four and dark from Jewish stock, he carried a bit too much weight for his heart. Trouble was, it looked good on him and he knew it. So, he was hardly encouraged to do anything sensible about it. A ready smile from dark brown eyes accompanied a spirited sense of humour. Whatever the occasion, he always dressed in a white collarless shirt and faded jeans, together with a full length, fawn coloured, camel hair coat and light brown, suede casual shoes. With his neatly trimmed curly black hair, he always looked the part, whatever part he was doing.

'I understand you're looking for furniture?' he spoke after sinking a third of his pint and wiping his lips with his right hand fingers and thumb.

'And pictures.' I replied.

'How much?' he watched me as he spoke. In fact in hindsight, I don't think he took his eyes off me, throughout our conversation.

'You mean how much furniture?'

'No,' he replied sipping his drink. 'How much money do you want to spend?'

'A couple of hundred grand.' I thought that would impress him, but it didn't seem to.

'I charge five percent and a further two point five if I have to travel abroad. Plus expenses.'

I'd expected something like that. 'Fine. I agree.' I can't believe I had made that decision without talking to Becky. He must have read my thoughts.

'Good. When can I see the house? Meet your wife – Becky isn't it?'

He'd obviously been briefed by our mutual friend. 'How about now?'

He nodded, so finished our beer we went out to the car park.

'Is it far?' he asked.

'Five minutes, no more.' I said.

'I'll follow you.' He went across to a silver Aston Martin, I got in our Volvo Estate. We drove the couple of miles, arriving home at about eight pm. I introduced him to Becky. She was fifteen years younger than me, but it had never been an issue. We all walked round both the inside and outside of our house.

It's a Dutch barn conversion. We'd found it while holidaying in the area two years ago. Buying it with five acres of land, together with the conversion work, had cost us the best part of four hundred thousand. Adding the furniture and art would see off nearly half of Becky's inheritance from her father. However, we'd agreed that from the start. As with most things, Becky and I were 'together' about the house. The windfall hadn't been a surprise. Her dad had told us both over a meal, two months before he died. It was a shame he couldn't have seen this house. He'd have loved it.

'Nice,' Jack said. We were on the rear patio, with the outside lighting on. Behind was our next project in it's infancy; a large hole where the swimming pool would be. 'With the figure you mentioned, I can sort you out a treat.'

'Good. How long?' I asked. Becky, who'd gone inside to make coffee, would want to know.

'Depends. For the furniture a week, maybe ten days. The pictures may take a bit longer, depending on what you want.'

Looking back, that was the nearest to hesitation I ever saw from Jack Davies.

Becky and I had planned a break to the Lake District that weekend. It was the first time we had been away since we bought the site. On our return on the Monday, there was a message from Jack on the answer phone.

'Call me. I might have something to interest you.'

I rang straight away.

'Can you get over here?' He told me where he was. I said we'd be there in an hour. Again I'd presumed upon Becky, but she was okay with it. We left the suitcases in the hall and drove to Jack's place.

It turned out to be a unit on a trading estate, just off the motorway. His car parked outside, helped with location. We entered a tiny office. Jack and I shook hands and he kissed Becky on the cheek. I watched her, but she didn't seem to mind, so neither did I.

'See what you both think of this.' Jack led us through a door into the main area of the unit. It was full of furniture. Good antique furniture at first glance. 'A client sold his country pile to move abroad. The buyers – Arabs – don't want any of this. I've got a good deal. You're looking at around seventy thou for the lot. That'll leave you a bit extra for pictures.'

For the next half hour Becky, Jack and I looked at and talked furniture. He was right, it was nice stuff. Mind I'm no expert, but Becky seemed to know a bit. She never ceases to surprise me. It turned out, that with the exception of two dinning chairs, everything was genuine.

'The table easily seats fourteen,' Jack said, 'maybe someone had two made to make up the numbers. They're good for 'repro' mind.'

We agreed. I said we'd talk about it tonight and ring him first thing tomorrow.

'Okay. No problem.' Jack waved us off as we left for home.

It turned out we had nothing to discuss, Becky and I. Moving around the house that evening, we 'placed' each piece.

'Don't wait until tomorrow, let's ring him now.'

Becky was impatient to make a decision. I knew the signs.

'That's good,' Jack said after I'd phoned him with our decision. 'I'll get it cleaned and polished and sort out delivery.'

Two weeks passed before we heard from him again. I spent three days in London, sorting some business. I work from home in the IT sector, but occasionally personal contact is essential. While I was there, I walked through Bond Street, looking at pictures in the many gallery's, getting a feel for what was around and at what price.

'You shouldn't have done that,' Becky said at dinner on the night I got home. 'You'll frighten yourself. Bond Street prices are always high.'

'I just wanted to get an idea of what's what.' I defended. The door bell rang. 'We're not expecting anyone are we?' I asked.

Becky had gone to answer it. 'It's Jack,' she said, showing him in.

'Sorry to interrupt your meal, I was just passing. I was going to ring you tomorrow anyway.' He was his usual ebullient self, but for the first time, I was suspicious about him. Nothing I'd go 'out on a limb' over, just something not quite right.

'I've found some picture. Or rather, where there are some that will suit you both.'

Becky and I looked at each other. On the first evening that we'd met Jack, we spoken to him of our likes and dislikes when it came to art.

He went on. 'There is a sale in Amsterdam next Tuesday and Wednesday. All sorts. I got them to send me a catalogue. You'll see, I've marked a few I think might be right up your street.'

For the next half an hour, we ate chocolate cake, drank coffee and talked art. Or should I say Becky and Jack talked art. I know what I like, Becky knows a bit more about art. We reached agreement on six pictures for sure, with another two maybes.

'So what happens now?' I asked Jack. 'You go and buy it next week.'

'No. it will cost you another two and a half percent if I go abroad.' He smiled at me. 'It will have to be one of you. Or we could telephone bid.'

Becky looked at me. 'I'll go.'

I thought for a moment. Why not? I was busy after my London trip. She'd be fine. Anyway, after the way that I had dominated the furniture buying, she could do the art.

'Sounds good to me.' I said. Her eyes said thank you.

So, there you are. A week later and I'm home alone. I had driven her to the airport and waved her off. An hour after I got home, she'd rung. She was in her hotel and was going to have a bath then an early night.

I'd been working in my office for a while, when the outside lights flicked on. They tend to be a bit sensitive, a cat had set them off the other day. I glanced up at the panel on the security control box. The green light in the French windows circuit came on. Getting up from my desk, I went quietly through to the hall and turned left into the lounge. There was a figure standing inside the window, silhouetted against the outside lights. It was obvious who it was. I switched the room lights on.

'Jack! What the heck do you think you are doing? Why didn't you ring the front door bell?'

I had just walked past him to shut the windows, when he swung at my head with something he was holding. Good reflexes saved me. I pulled away as a piece of 'four by two' hissed past my right ear. Having lost the element of surprise, Jack was no match for me. I hit him once on the chin and he was down on the floor. Dragging him too a chair I tied him up, then sat down opposite, waiting for him to recover conscience.

When he finally woke, he didn't want to talk. I went into the kitchen and rang our mutual friend. Over the next few minutes he told me why, a few weeks ago, he had thought I must have known Jack Davies. I rang off, made a cup of coffee and returned to the lounge.

'So whose idea was it Jack, yours or Becky's?'

At the mention of her name, he looked at me through narrowed eyes, but didn't answer.

'You had your chance with her years ago, so why now.' They'd been an item before I came on the scene, according to our friend. Still he didn't speak.

'Forbidden fruits. Of course, that's what it is. So who's idea was Amsterdam? No. don't tell me, Becky's. You fool Jack. She's hung you out to dry. If the plan worked, fine. If it didn't, she's got the alibi.'

I crossed to the French doors and looked out. There was a fresh hole in the bottom of the pool. Of course. The concrete for the base was coming tomorrow. Simple.

It was Jack's name that Becky called out, when she came through the front door two days later. I'd left his car on the drive. She assumed things had gone according to her plan. I waited by the open French windows, looking at the hole I had just dug, where the diving platform would eventually be.

The Sweet Smell of Scorn

Jenny spent the first day after David left, packing the remains of her life into cardboard boxes, black bags and suitcases. She quite simply had not seen it coming. He'd given absolutely no indication of being unhappy with her. Then right out of the blue, he had telephoned yesterday from his office. He was leaving her. Yes! There was someone else. Yes! It had been going on for a while. No! He wouldn't be home last night. It was for the best. In a few days, he would come and collect his things.

Day two, she had the removal company come and collect her belongings. Then she spent hours cleaning everywhere. All of his things she left, exactly where she found them. That evening she sat down for the last time, at the beautiful dining room table. She lit candles, put on some soft music and feasted on a pound of shrimp, a jar of caviar and a bottle of Chardonnay, that she drank from a chipped china mug. When she had finished her meal, Jackie went into every room and deposited a few half-eaten shrimp shells dipped in caviar, into the hollow of every curtain rail. The next morning she packed her bedding, and a few odd bits and pieces into her car, cleaned the kitchen and left.

David brought his new girlfriend Anna home a couple of days later. They were surprised to find Jackie wasn't there, and so decided to move in. All was fine to start with. Then slowly the house began to smell. They looked everywhere. Then cleaned, scrubbed and aired the place out. They checked for dead rodents. The carpets were steam cleaned. Air fresheners hung everywhere. A firm of exterminators came and set off gas canisters. During that time, David and Anna went to her old flat for a few days. Finally, they replaced all the expensive woollen carpets. Nothing made the slightest difference.

People stopped coming to visit. Repairmen refused to work in the house. Their cleaning lady left. Finally, they couldn't tolerate the stench any longer. The decision was made to move. They put the house onto the market. A month passed and even though they had brought down their price by almost half, they could not find a buyer for their smelly house. Word had quite obviously got out and eventually, even the local estate agent refused to return their calls. They were left with no alternative, but to negotiated a huge mortgage to purchase their new house.

Jenny rang David and asked how things were going. He recounted to her the whole awful saga. She listened in silence, then told him how much she missed the old home. She offered to reduce the divorce settlement in exchange for getting the house back. Knowing she couldn't possibly understand how bad the smell was, David agreed on a price that was about a quarter of what the house had originally been worth. But only if they completed the paperwork that very day. Jenny agreed. Within three hours, his lawyers had delivered the paperwork to her, and she in turn had signed.

David and Anna spent the next few days, packing everything they could from the house. A week later, they both stood smiling, as the removal company took the whole lot to their new home. The whole lot of course, included every single curtain rod.

The Brown Paper Package

Charles Aloysius Winston Henderson stood beneath the canopy that covered his fruit and vegetable stall. The rain had been falling for two days without any apparent end in sight. In that time, it had become almost as wet under the canopy as outside, what with the wind blowing rain straight in and a split in the top tarpaulin that defied permanent repair.

Two hours ago he had collected the stall from the lockup where it spent nights, then pushed it two hundred yards to his pitch on Gladys Road. There, he'd arranged the fruit and vegetables that he had bought down at the market earlier that morning. Now it was 8.00am., five hours after he'd left his one bedroom flat and he was set up, ready for the day.

'Tea Charlie?' Tom Peters called out as he walked by.

'Ta mate. Lovely.' It was a daily ritual, Tom had a stall about fifty yards up the road. The café was thirty yards the other way. So Tom got breakfast each day.

'Wad?'

'Bacon.' Charlie called out to Tom's fast disappearing head.

'No egg?'

Charlie didn't eat eggs. Nor did he ever reply to Tom's daily question, more than to smile a little. Tom never saw those smiles.

Ten minutes passed and Tom returned. He handed

Charlie a paper bag and a plastic cup with a lid. Charlie gave him some coins. 'What's all this?' Tom was looking down at his hand.

'One twenty for today, and one thirty five for Saturday.' Charlie said. 'Remember? I didn't have no change.'

'And I told you not to leave the country. Right. Ta.' Tom took the plastic top off his cup carefully. 'See the kids yesterday?'

'Nah. Their Gran takes them off to the cinema once a month.' Charlie and his wife had separated three years ago. Better friends now than they'd ever been when together, if there was one thing they agreed about, it was where the children were concerned. Six year old Katy and four year old Simon were blissfully unaware of their parents difficulties with each other.

'You? Gunners I suppose.'

Tom supported Arsenal. 'Where they home? Is the Pope Catholic?'

Both men smiled, Charlie raised his eyebrows a little, 'win?'

'Of course.' Tom unwrapped the cellophane off a pack of twenty cigarettes and passed one to his friend. With a wave of his hand, he was gone. They would meet later at the 'Angel'.

For the next four hours, Charlie worked the stall. He had sort of inherited it from his Mum, she from her Dad. For fifty or more years, there had been Henderson's on the market. Grandpa Henderson had arrived in London with his wife and five year old daughter – Charlie's mum – from Jamaica at the end of the war. Brought over to work on the buses, he'd stuck it for a few years. Then, when a stall came available on the local market and in spite of there being opposition to a Jamaican having a licence, Aloysius Henderson had prevailed. He'd retired in 1970 and his daughter had carried the on. She met someone in the early sixties. It didn't work out for them, but Charlie was born. She never told the father, never needed to. She named her baby for Prince Charles, her father and Churchill. She never abbreviated it, always Charles.

They had been out at the far end of the market, beyond Tom's present site to start with. But as people died or moved on, so the Henderson's risen up the 'pecking order'. It was important to have got to where their 'pitch' was now, because it put them at the junction of Gladys Road and the High Street. So much more passing trade. Charlie Henderson and his family before him had paid their dues.

Across the High Street opposite the end of the stalls, was the Angel and Crown, the market pub. At 12.30 pm, with his mother looking after the stall as she always did, Charlie went for his lunch. He crossed the High Street and entered the Public Bar. Tom was already there. He saw Charlie enter.

'My shout Chas mate. What's yours?'

'Usual thanks.'

The publican saw Tom and nodded. 'With you in a tick, Tom.' The routine was a daily one, for as far back as most of them wanted to remember. A few moments later, the two friends sat with their pint glasses half emptied, as they washed away the mornings dryness from their mouths, caused by constant chat with the customers.

'Still raining,' Charlie said, a statement rather than a question.

Tom nodded. 'Probably go on for a few more days yet. Global warming is what's causing all of this, d'ya know?'

'Rot. It's much warmer in Jamaica, and it doesn't rain all the time.' Charles watched his friend and took another good swallow of beer.

'True, you've got a point there mate. Hadn't thought of that.'

Both men sat quietly, drinking. Charlie got the second pints in and twenty minutes later, having finished, they both left the Angel to get back to work.

'Hello Mrs. H. Okay?' Tom said as they reached Charlie's stall.

'Hello Thomas. I'm well thank you, and yourself?'

Tom smiled and held a thumb up to her. 'See ya Chas mate.'

'Yeh, see ya.'

Mother and son chatted for a few minutes, and then Mrs Henderson prepared to leave. 'Do you need anything from the shops? I'm going now,' she said.

'No ta,' Charlie put some tomatoes in a bag as he spoke. They were for a customer who stood dripping in the rain. He swung the paper bag between his fingers and handed it across. '85p luv?'

His mother disappeared along the High Street.

'I'm sorry, I've only got a twenty pound note.'

'It's all money.' Charlie said. 'No problem, I've plenty of change.' Charlie sorted out some notes and coin and handed it over. 'There you go, luv.'

'Thanks,' there was a flash of a smile from her and she was gone.

Charlie sat on a stool at the back of the stall, and started to bag up some of the money in his waist pouch. All notes went into a wallet, that had been his grandad's. He finished sorting out the morning's takings, then sat deep in thought about nothing in particular for a few minutes. Then he saw a brown package under the stall. Reaching down to pick it up, he saw it was a paper bag, like they used on the stall. Mum must have dropped it he thought as he opened it and looked inside.

'Jeez,' he said out loud. He screwed the bag shut, looking around to see if anyone had heard. Nothing. Opening it again, he pulled out a handful of fifty pound notes. Checking once more that no-one was watching, he counted them quickly. They were blue paper banded into three lots of twenty and there was a loose ten. Three and a half grand.

Charlie put them back in the bag and into his inside jacket pocket. He sat back down to think. For the package to have got where it was, only his mother could have dropped it. An artificial grass curtain and various boxes would prevent it from coming in from the front of the stall. So, what was she doing with all this money? Why keep it in a paper bag? Why be so careless as to lose it?

The rest of the day passed too slowly by far. All Charlie wanted to do was get home, 'phone Mum, sort this out. Five o'clock finally came and he pushed his stall to the lockup. A quick sweep up around the pitch, and having collected his van, he headed for home. Arriving there, he shrugged out of his wet coat and jacket and having put the package on the kitchen tablet, he filled the kettle.

His mother answered her phone after the sixth ring.

'Hello, who's that?' she said, inquiringly.

'Mum?'

'Hello Charles. Is that you? What are you calling for?'

'Mum, have you lost something?'

'Lost something do you say? I don't think so.'

'Something in a brown bag?'

'I haven't got a brown bag.'

'A brown paper bag, like we use on the stall.'

'Will you stop talking in riddles Charles. Get to the point.'

'Mum, I found some money in a bag under the stall. I thought it must be yours.'

'Money? Mine? I am more careful than that with my money.'

'Mum, it's three and a half grand.' He almost whispered the figure.

'How much?' Mrs Henderson's voice blasted her son's eardrum. 'Where do you suppose I would get that sort of money from?'

'I don't know Mum.' Charlie thought for a moment. She was right. They managed, always had. But they'd never been what some might call 'flush with money'.

'Charles Henderson, you bring that money round here, right this instant. Do you hear me?'

'OK Mum. I'll just have a wash, get changed and be with you in half an hour.' He replaced the phone on it's cradle. Half an hour later, and he arrived at his mothers house. He locked the van and went down the path to the front door. She must have been watching out for him, because it was already open.

'Wipe your feet,' she said as he entered. That was her normal greeting to anyone who came into her house, as she herself was disappearing down the corridor towards her kitchen. Charlie followed. It was warm and familiar. He handed the bag across to his mother and sat down at the table. She placed the bag carefully on her side of the table, then poured them both some tea.

'It is all here Charles? she said quietly after sitting

down. 'There isn't more that you are not telling me about?'

'I'm not bothering to answer that Mother.' Charlie was hurt she would say anything like that. 'You know me better.'

'I have never known you with three and a half thousand pounds before.' She reached for the bag as she spoke.

'And that isn't yours?' Charlie asked quietly, nodding at the bag.

'Never set eyes on it 'till now.' Mrs. Henderson opened the bag slowly and peered inside. Then, even more slowly, she raised her eyes until she was looking straight at her son.

'What?' Charlie looked at her. 'What's up?'

Without a word, his mother handed the open bag across the table. Charlie snatched it from her hand and looked inside. The contents had clearly started life as a cheese and tomato sandwich, secured in cling-film. It was looking slightly crushed, but was probably still edible. Charles Aloysius Winston Henderson sat quietly thinking for a couple of moments, then getting slowly to his feet he left the house, returned to his car and drove home.

His mother watched her only son – forever the dreamer – leave, without calling out to him.

The Wonders of Education

The sun shone through a row of poplar trees, casting shadows that almost exactly coincided with the stripes of the zebra crossing. Crossing the High Street, Tom Rhodes noticed the symmetry. He entered his local library, heading up towards the first floor and the reference section. Collecting a copy of the local paper from a rack, he settled down in his usual chair beside a window, through which warm sunlight streamed. He read the job vacancies pages, making occasional notes on a pad he had brought with him.

Twenty minutes passed. He stretched and felt a little drowsy. When he thought about it some time later, he wasn't sure whether he had in fact dozed off before first seeing the little old man.

'Good mornin' to yuz sur,'

Tom couldn't pin the accent right down.

'If you don't mind me sayin', yuz lookin a bit dreamy sur.'

He was quite obviously ancient, though brisk movements belied his years. His hair and beard were white and full, his crinkled face pink. A twinkle lived permanently in his green eyes. He wore a brown, rough tweed suit with a green silk waistcoat, red spotted bow tie and brown leather brogues. Tom's attention was caught by the way the old man sat cross legged on top of the table, and that he was – quite obviously – only three feet tall.

Looking around to check that he was alone, as usual at this time of day, Tom felt comfortable about replying. 'Good morning. Do I?'

'Yes sur, so yuz do. Now sur, my name is Fergal. Is there somethin' I could be helpin' ya with sur?'

Tom looked at the old man, finding himself warming towards him. 'I don't know. I am trying to find a change of direction, a new job. Something to get my brain going again.' Tom found himself telling Fergal how he had been made redundant six months ago. 'I was an accountant up at the car factory on the outside of town. I'd been there for twenty eight years. So I've come here today at the suggestion of the Job Centre to broaden my horizons, widen my parameters. After all, I'm only forty eight, I still feel employable – just.'

'I see sur.' Fergal said when Tom had finished. 'Well, it must be yuz lucky day. Helping folks out with that sort of thing, is right up my street.'

'How do you mean?' Tom wasn't certain about any of this.

'I'll just nip off and get yuz a couple of books sur. Just to give an idea about what's available. Be back in two shakes of a weasel's tail.'

With a whoosh he was gone, returning seconds later with another whoosh. He settled back down onto the table, crossed his legs and handed Tom three books, identical except for their titles. 'There ya go sur. Ya have a good look at those, see if they be the sort of ting, what yuz after.'

Tom read the titles. 'Self Sufficiency from a Grow-Bag', 'Gourmet Tripe Cuisine' and 'Build a Computer from Kitchen Scraps.' Smiling, he handed them back to Fergal. 'They are not quite what I had in mind.'

'I'm sorry sur. Indeed I am. Was it startin' a business,

that's attracting yuz?' Before Tom could answer Fergal had gone again, to return seconds later with six more similar books.

He handed Tom three of them. 'Are those more the kind of thing sur?'

Tom could hardly believe his eyes at the titles. 'Ball Point Pen Maintenance Course', 'Profiting from Insomnia', and 'Sparrow Farming – the Facts'. Did he laugh or cry? What was happening? He could still feel the warm sun on his face. It must be really happening to him.

Fergal spoke again. 'If ya don't mind me sayin' sur, yuz not lookin' too happy. Have I still not got it quite right sur?'

Tom shook his head. 'No, it's not that Fergal. I just don't understand any of this.'

'Bless yuz sur, of course ya don't. That's why ya be wantin' some educatin'. D'ya see sur, yuz a smart man and that's for sure. It's just well, ya be needin' some fresh ideas, so yuz do.'

'And you think that these books are fresh ideas, do you?' Tom was laughing at the thought, almost as much as he was at the books.

'Look at these then sur. They may well be the answer.' Fergal handed over the other three books. Tom saw that they too were identical except for their titles. He read them out aloud.

''House Training Mongolian Fruit Bats', 'The DIY Guide to Draft Proofing Bird Cages' and 'The Flat Hunting Guide for Devil Worshippers'.'

'Ya read fair beautiful sur," Fergal said, hugging his legs. "It's fair brung tears to me eye's.'

Tom too was in tears, he couldn't speak for laughter. It was several moment before he recovered control.

"Where are you getting these books from?' He said, finally able to speak.

'They're here, there and everywhere sur.' Now Fergal's eyes were really twinkling.

'I'm dreaming all of this, aren't I?' Tom said. "I'll wake up in a moment, and it'll end.' He tried to shake himself back to reality. Nothing happened.

'I don't think so sur. Yuz in need of help, that's for sure. I can change all of those books if ya want.' Without waiting for Tom to answer, he gathered them up and was gone. He returned in a flash with another selection. 'Can you read out loud again, if ya please, sur?'

'Why?' Tom asked, looking at the tiny man. 'Can't you read them for yourself?'

'It' could be somethin' of that sort, sur.' Fergal winked knowingly.

Tom read the latest titles that had been brought out aloud. ''How to start a Range War', 'The Collectors Guide to Sardine Tin Keys', 'The Wok Cook Book for Sinophobics.''

Tom nearly fell off his chair laughing. Fergal rolled around on the table, though he was laughing at Tom. Finally, they both regained control.

'What's a Range War sur?' Fergal asked.

Tom spent a moment or two, trying to explain.

'That's all right then. Looks like I've hit the spot, this time sur.' Fergal said. 'Which one are ya going to go for?'

Tom shook his head. 'You can't seriously expect me to choose one of these. Surely, they're all just a joke.'

'Depends on what ya mean by a joke sur.' The little man scratched vigorously at his beard. Tom found himself thinking that something weird and wonderful might work loose and fall out.

Then, in a flash, the books were gathered together and once more Fergal was gone. Only for a second or two, before he was back with three more.

'What have you brought this time, you old rascal?' Tom was smiling even before he reached for the latest books. ' 'Word Games for the Dyslexic', 'The Complete Schizophrenic' and 'The Government White Paper Colouring Book'.'

They both collapsed laughing, out of control for quite some time. Tears poured down their cheeks. Fergal might well have fallen off the table, if Tom hadn't pushed him back on. Then they sat for a moment, just looking at each other.

Finally Tom broke the silence. 'Are you going to tell me what this is all about, Fergal?'

'If yuz wantin' me to, sur. It's all about Tom Rhodes. Surely yuz clever enough to work that out?'

'How do you know my name? I haven't told you, have I?' Tom realised that he wasn't even completely certain about that.

Fergal got up and walked right round the table top. Arriving back from where he'd started, sat down and re-crossed his legs.

'Such small things sur. Such small questions. Yuz worryin' about all the wrong things. Just concentrate on the big things, that's for sure.'

'House training a Mongolian fruit bat. That's your idea of a big thing?' Tom shook his head, dismissing the answer, even before he'd heard it.

'Everythin's big from where I am sittin', sur.' Fergal's eyes had taken on an extra twinkle. 'If ya owned a Mongolian fruit bat sur, house trainin' it would take on a whole new importance for yuz.. I don't know if ya can make a livin' out of the doing of it sur. But for sure, it would be great fun trying.'

'So that's what this is all about is it, Fergal.' Tom spoke quietly as things began to dawn on him. "You think I need to relax; see the funny side of life a bit more.'

As he spoke, Fergal and the books where nowhere to be seen. Tom wondered if he had been asleep, dreamt it all; though It didn't feel like it. He folded the newspaper, returned it to the rack, and went downstairs to the ground floor, and crossed to the exit. He stopped for a moment, then turned back to the inquiry desk.

The duty librarian was a middle aged man. "Can I help you, sir?'

'I don't know,' Tom said thoughtfully. 'Have you got a book titled 'The Flat Hunting Guide for Devil Worshippers?''

The man typed on a keyboard, before studying a computer screen. 'No, sorry. There doesn't appear to be any such title. Do you know the author's name?' he asked.

Tom thought, then replied with a wry smile, 'I think so, but not his last name.'

'You're sure about the title?' The librarian was still searching the data base. 'It just seems a bit funny to me.'

Tom chuckled, 'I think yuz just hit the nail on it's proverbial head.' With a nod of thanks, he left the library, smiling and whistling.

Printed in the United Kingdom
by Lightning Source UK Ltd.
114971UKS00001B/136-186